Contents

Destroyer

Andrew Hickey

BY THE SAME AUTHOR:

- Sci-Ence! Justice Leak!

- The Beatles In Mono

- The Beach Boys On CD: vol 1 - 1961-1969

- The Beach Boys On CD: vol 2 - 1970-2011

- An Incomprehensible Condition:An Unauthorised Guide To Grant Morrison's Seven Soldiers

- Monkee Music

- Preservation: The Kinks' Music 1964-1974

- Ideas and Entities

- California Dreaming: The LA Pop Music Scene and the 1960s

- Faction Paradox: Head of State

- The Black Archive: The Mind Robber

- Welcome to the Multiverse: An Unauthorised Guide to Grant Morrison's Multiversity (ebook only)

- Fifty Stories for Fifty Years: An Unauthorised Look at Doctor Who

For Holly

Chapter 1

May 1941. A cold, dark, night. The pilot is determined that the plane will reach its target, bearing a cargo that could determine the course of the war, and the fate of the entire planet. Maybe even more than that. Nothing is more important than this. Not even the pilot's own life. His life, after all, is only that of one man, and he has already decided to put it in service of the greatest possible cause. If he loses it, so be it. There are worse things than death. And he, who has been so willing to send others to their deaths, can't balk at the idea of his own.

May is supposed to be a warm month. A month when the days are finally growing noticeably longer after a long, dark, winter, when the sun is finally up long enough to heat the ground below. A month when you can feel the flowers bursting from the ground, and everything coming to life. May is meant to be spring.

But flying across the North Sea, at night, in a one-man plane, is cold no matter what the time of year, and the pilot can see his own breath in the air. He shivers, and smells the aeroplane fuel, a scent that fills him full of wonder, even as the fumes make him slightly dizzy. The aeroplane is a marvel of modernity, of Aryanism. It is the greatest marvel of a century of wonders. The plane allows a man to fly above the world and, if necessary, to rain death down upon it. The aeroplane is everything that National Socialism is working towards – soon the whole world will be controlled by those who create such

machines. The future that is coming is one where such techno-
logical marvels will be commonplace. But that future depends
on his actions tonight.

The Reich and Britain should not be enemies. The Aryan
race should not be divided. The pilot knows this, deep in his
heart. The two great empires should be allies against the Communist threat. All other concerns should be secondary to that.
And his great work would bring the day of peace closer. All he
has to do – all that the golden future requires of him – is to
get his plane to Scotland. After that, he can rest. His job will
be done.

That would be a simple task in most circumstances, but
right now there is a war raging in Europe – a war that the pilot
hopes to end, but which may take his life before he has the
chance. Not only will the enemy attack him if they can, but his
own side may not realise the nature of the mission with which
he has been entrusted. They, too, may attempt to kill him.
They may even succeed.

No matter. He is only one man. Millions have died already.
And millions more will die before this is all over. His only task
is to ensure that those millions will be the enemies of the Reich,
and that they are a sacrifice for the best of causes.

It is the darkest of nights, in the darkest of times, but the
pilot is bringing the light. Soon this conflict will be over, and
soon the glory of the German people will be obvious to all.
This fallen world will rise up again, and become worthy of the
Führer's genius. It will come through the fire and be purged
of its impurities, the pure metal fit to be forged into the shape
the Führer has anticipated.

The twentieth century is the German century, and the pilot
knows it. He is the bearer of a cargo as important to the future
of the world as the Holy Grail itself. He is Parsifal, carrying the
spear that will heal the wounds in the Aryan people and unite
them against their common foe. His plane, like that spear, is
a weapon that does not serve the purpose of weapons. It will

unify rather than tear apart.

The cargo is only a handful of documents, but what documents they are! They are the culmination of his life's work. The pilot had never been the most ardent of mystics – his devotion to the cause is a personal one, not an ideological one – but nonetheless, he understands the import of this moment. It may well be the most important moment in the history of the world. He feels genuinely humble, even while acknowledging his own role in history. He is not the important one. He is just a vessel.

The documents he is carrying will change everything. Given to the Reich's allies, they will allow the civilised world to unite against the lesser men, the dwarves who are determined to destroy everything good about civilisation. His allies are noble men. They will know what to do with them.

The storm rages around him. He's dizzy now. His heart is racing with excitement, and the blood is rushing in his ears so loudly it almost drowns out the sound of the plane's engines. He bites his lip, and feels the salt, metallic taste of his blood in his mouth mingle with the smell of the plane fuel. He closes his eyes, just for a second, and allows himself to become one with the plane, to feel what it feels, to experience the air rushing around him and the ground pulling him towards it. To know the freedom of the air, and realise that it is only with a superhuman effort that such freedom can be maintained.

The pilot knows this mission, the most important of his life, must succeed. He has been entrusted with this mission by the Führer, and no-one else can possibly know its true purpose. Even Rudolf Hess, himself, the pilot, doesn't know all the details, although he is the one who oversaw it all personally. He desperately needs to see the Duke of Hamilton, the only man he can trust. He needs to get the documents to him, and to relieve himself of this immense burden.

The plane starts to head towards the ground. Hess knows that the plane will not survive the landing, but he is sure that he will remain unharmed. The hand of destiny is on his shoulder.

Chapter 2

"Bored, bored, bored, bored, bored"

Bletchley Park was a beautiful house, with exquisite grounds, but the hundreds of people labouring away in the huts in those grounds scarcely had time to stop and look at them for a second. There was work to be done – work that could easily make the difference in the war effort, and save countless lives. Because Bletchley Park was where some of the most secret work of the war was taking place – the decryption of German military messages.

The people working on that exceptional task were not, to look at them, exceptional people, and in that respect at least Alan Turing was not unusual. He was of average height, though he looked shorter, due to a tendency to attempt to fade into the background. He was twenty-eight, but looked younger, and no matter how much he tried to control his hair, it would look ruffled within a couple of hours. He looked utterly typical of the mathematicians who were working in Bletchley, but for his eyes, which were a piercing blue which stood out dramatically against his otherwise dark colouring.

He wouldn't have said as much to anyone else, of course – modesty would forbid it – but Turing knew that he was, if not the most intelligent man in the country, certainly the most intelligent man involved in the espionage community. He had already made some of the most important conceptual breakthroughs in mathematics in generations.

And on this day in May, the greatest mathematical mind in Europe was sitting in an office which, no matter what the weather outside, was always slightly too chilly for comfort, looking at yet another tedious piece of paperwork that needed to be filled in with the results of a meeting he had attended more or less against his will.

"When I was brought in to this job, I was told I'd be a mathematician, not a bloody, buggering, administrator. I'm supposed to have important mathematical work to do, but instead all I do is have meetings about meetings about meetings!"

Talking to himself had become a habit in recent months, as the need for intelligent conversation came into conflict with the necessity of secrecy. Secrecy was not something Turing was particularly suited for, either by training or temperament; he was a mathematician, and mathematics, like all the sciences and indeed every aspect of human culture and knowledge, grew by sharing ideas and building on what came before. More importantly even than that, he was a man who knew that a secret can never be entirely kept, and that the incorrect belief that one has successfully hidden something can be much more harmful than the public exposure of a secret ever could. His work showed that – the Nazis believed their encryption kept their secrets safe.

Turing knew that Newton's comment about standing on the shoulders of giants was meant as an insult, aimed at a short rival, but he also knew that there was truth in it. Only by sharing knowledge could mathematics ever progress – Newton himself had provided the perfect counterexample, by keeping calculus to himself until Leibniz reinvented it independently, and thus got all the glory.

He saw the need for secrecy in his current work, of course – it would hardly do to tell the Germans "Oh, by the way, we're reading all your most secret communications, and know what you're planning to do next" – but like so many of the irritants in his life, that need was a contingent fact caused by the stupidity and irrationality of the human race, rather than a fundamental of the universe.

The basic job of breaking the Enigma code had been completed long ago. Now it had almost become routine – gather the transmissions every day, try to find a crib as quickly as possible, run them through the machines. There was little intellectual satisfaction in that kind of work.

Turing was still an important part of the work – possibly the most important, he liked to think – but it was no longer the mathematical and engineering puzzle that he'd been drawn to in the early months of the war. And while for the most part that was a good thing, there was a tiny, selfish part of him that missed that work.

And so Turing had, instead, become an administrator. It had happened piecemeal, but by now it had become unmistakable. He was doing important, necessary, vital work – but not *his* work. It wasn't that he objected to the work itself, of course, no matter how tedious – he was very aware that there were men all over the world dying, while he was sat in an (admittedly chilly, admittedly dull) office, and he never forgot how comparatively lucky he was. But still. It was dull.

He gazed, half-reading, at the documents before him. The subjects were all personnel matters, organisational, bureaucratic – everything that required the maximum thought for the minimal intellectual pleasure. He chewed on his pencil while trying to bring himself to think properly, and then grimaced at the next sip of tea as he realised there were tiny flecks of wood in his mouth.

The phone rang, the piercing noise once again breaking his concentration while he was trying to drink his mug of tea. Not that the tea was actually any good – institutional tea has its own flavour, as if someone had put a pair of sweaty socks into the urn. Turing imagined at times that he could almost see the socks in his mind's eye. They would be grey, woollen ones, and would have been worn for a full weekend's walking through particularly muddy fields, in leaky boots. Possibly a few cowpats would also have been involved.

But still, a man needed his tea if he wanted to have any chance of getting his brain to work properly. Not that his brain was needed for these papers, of course.

He sighed, and reached for the phone.

"Not a moment's peace around here. Hello, who is it?"

"It's Godfrey here. Not busy, are you? Only something rather important has come up. I'd like you to go and see Fleming."

Chapter 3

Turing had never been in this office before, but it wasn't as if any of the offices in Bletchley were radically different from each other anyway. While the main hall was pretty enough, in an ostentatious sort of way, the surrounding buildings were functional rather than beautiful.

The same could be said for the rather angular-looking man with the beaky nose in front of him, looking at him through eyes which seemed permanently half-closed. Nobody would ever call *him* beautiful, but at the same time there was an air of confidence from him, as if he knew exactly what his purpose in life was, and so could go through his existence with no further worry. He looked a little older than Turing, and a little taller, but those few years and inches seemed to have given him the confidence that Turing had always lacked. He was clearly in his element, and Turing envied him immensely.

"Mr. Turing?"

"Doctor Turing, actually."

"I do beg your pardon, *Doctor* Turing. My name's Ian Fleming."

"We've met."

"Have we? Oh, that's right! I've seen you around Bletchley before. Do take a seat. Drink?"

"Not at this time of day, thank you. I like to keep a clear head for my work."

"Suit yourself. Personally, I find having a clear head a dreadful handicap. You don't mind if I do, though?"

"No, go ahead."

Fleming got up and walked over to a small cabinet, from which he removed a bottle of whisky and a glass. He poured himself a small measure, tipped the bottle half-way back to vertical, then stopped, gazed thoughtfully at the bottle, and seemed to make a decision. He poured again, giving himself a large double, before replacing the bottle, closing the cabinet, and sitting back down. He took a sip, and paused for a second to savour the taste.

He seemed to compose his thoughts, and then asked almost casually, "Has the news about Hess permeated to the general public yet?"

"What news about Hess?"

"Ah, that's what I thought. It'll be all over the news in a few hours, I'm sure. Do you know who Rudolf Hess is?"

"Of course. Hitler's second in command."

"Well, technically. He's been more or less pushed aside as the war's gone on, in favour of Goering and Goebbels. Anyway, he's in Britain right now."

"You mean he's defected? Good God!"

"Not defected, exactly. He's come over in the hope of making peace. Apparently as a rogue agent."

"Apparently?"

"Well, we know different. It was us who persuaded him to come over."

Fleming paused to appreciate the look of shock on Turing's face, and it took Turing a few moments to recover sufficiently to respond.

Eventually, however, he managed to ask the obvious next question. "How in the world did you do that?"

"Have you heard about The Link?"

"What link?"

"It's a group of rich Nazis. Mostly from the Mitford set, those sort of people."

"What sort of people are those? I'm sorry, I don't know who the Mitford set are."

Fleming gave a slight smirk, and hesitated a fraction of a second before replying.

"I do beg your pardon, Doctor Turing. One forgets sometimes that not everybody has society connections. You're rather better off not knowing who the Mitfords are, so I shall refrain from explanation. Just think of rich idiots who have a superficial, dilettantish interest in political dogmas – an interest which, while tissue-thin, is still stronger than their commitment to the country."

Turing nodded. "I think I know the sort."

"Anyway, some of those people are supporters of the Nazis, and it has suited our interests to have them believe we are unaware of this, while we feed them information. Hess didn't just decide to come here on a whim. We've been working on him for months, through various intermediaries. We've got him convinced that Britain wants peace with the Nazis on their terms. He thinks we're desperate to install a puppet government and become Berlin's slaves. Because we've told him that."

"Surely – surely! – no-one could really be that gullible. This is the second most important man in Germany. He can't have been taken in by a basic confidence trick, can he?"

"I think you're severely underestimating the gullibility of the Nazis. They're not known for their intelligence and discretion, you know."

"Even so!"

Fleming smiled. "I know you boffins think the rest of us are a bunch of fools who don't know anything – no, don't deny it, I've heard enough of your conversations – but there are skills in the world other than mathematics and fiddling with vacuum tubes."

Fleming walked over to a filing cabinet, unlocked it with a key taken from his inside jacket pocket, and pulled out a handful of papers. He flicked through them to make sure they were what he thought they were, extracted a couple of sheets, which he returned to the cabinet, and then handed the rest to Turing.

"Take a look at these. What do you think?"

The papers were covered with letters. They were handwritten, rather than typed, and clearly in a Germanic hand, but Turing recognised what he was looking at.

"It's a ciphertext of some sort, yes?"

"It is. If anything, you see, our plan has worked rather too well. Hess brought these papers over to share with the members of the Link. Now we need to know what they say."

"And it's not the standard Enigma code?"

"I'm afraid not. And we can't just turn this over to the girls in the huts. We need you to take personal responsibility for this. I, on the other hand, am going to take responsibility for Hess himself."

"Do you have any clues at all as to what kind of code it is?"

"Not at the moment. But I believe I can probably persuade Hess to give us a clue. In the meantime, though, I'd like you to do what you can, and let me know what you think."

Turing gathered the papers together, stood up, and left the room, forgetting even to nod to Fleming as he left. He was already planning his first line of investigation.

Chapter 4

The room was grey and functional, with little in it other than a bed with a grey, woollen, blanket and a single rather dejected pillow lying squashed on it. It had a shabby, Spartan, air about it, but would be relatively acceptable as a place to sleep. It was cold, of course, but so was everything at the moment. And at a time of rationing, keeping prisoners of war in comfort was not a top priority.

As cells went, Fleming thought, this one could be a lot more unpleasant. Rudolf Hess might be a prisoner of war, but he was also the second in command in the German government, and that apparently meant he deserved some respect. What Fleming thought he deserved, though, was a kick in the balls.

And those balls were inviting such a kick. The prisoner was lying on his bed, with his legs spread and pointed in the direction of the door through which Fleming had entered. Fleming looked down at the disgusting little man, with his receding hairline and thick eyebrows, and felt nothing but contempt for him.

"Stay civil," he reminded himself, "but make sure he knows who's in charge." After staring silently until the prisoner finally looked up, Fleming spoke.

"Prisoner Hess?"

"You will address me by my proper title."

"I will address you however I feel, you nasty little shitstain of a man. I'm here to talk about the papers, *Prisoner Hess.*" So the civility had not lasted particularly well.

"You are not the Duke of Hamilton. I do not talk to under-lings. I will only talk to Hamilton."

"I thought you wanted to negotiate peace?"

"I do."

"But only with Hamilton?"

"That is correct."

"Would you mind telling me why?"

"He is like myself. He is a flyer. An aviator. Those of us who have flown, who have seen what the world looks like from a higher plane, have a different perspective on the world from those of you who remain stuck to the ground."

"So you're willing to talk, but only to a pilot?"

"Not any pilot. I want Hamilton. Bring me Hamilton, or torture me for the information you want, but stop playing these games."

Fleming appeared to think for a while. In truth, he had already known that this would be Hess' attitude — he knew far more about Hess and his plan than the prisoner would ever realise. But he needed to appear ignorant in order to discover the few things he didn't already know.

Of course, it showed Hess' mindset that he immediately suspected that he would be tortured. Fleming didn't know what disgusted him more, the thought of torture or the thought that Hess had such a low opinion of the British. Of course, you'd occasionally have to smack a man around a little, put the boot in where it was needed, but *torture*? That was what the Nazis did, not the British Empire.

Fleming started to pace around the small room, noting the utter lack of anything to stimulate or enrich the mind. Were he to be cooped up in such a place, he'd find himself going crazy through boredom within a week. He sniffed, and had to suppress a gag reflex at the smell of a room whose single occupant hadn't washed in days, and hadn't left the room even to use the lavatory in the same period of time.

And how much worse must Hess be taking this? He was,

after all, someone who was used to the trappings of power, and was expecting to be treated like a hero upon reaching Britain. He would, Fleming had no doubt, be breaking very soon. Keep him off guard, don't let him get the measure of you. Polite, then angry, then polite again.

"Please explain why Hamilton is so important to you. He's a very busy man – surely another pilot would be acceptable?"

"No, I have spoken to Hamilton in the past, many years ago. He is a man of honour. I trust him. I do not trust your other pilots. They are not honourable."

Fleming turned toward Hess, eyes blazing with a fury he was only half pretending. This was his chance to see if he could make Hess snap altogether. His face grew red, and he towered over the still-prone prisoner.

"You *dare*? You *dare* to claim that Britain's pilots are not honourable? As if a Nazi could know anything at all about what honour means. You're lucky I don't smash your face in right now, you disgusting little wretch."

Hess cringed. The man was clearly a physical coward, for all his apparent bravery in flying solo to Britain. Someone who could easily be dominated by a more aggressive man. No wonder, Fleming thought, that he had fallen under Hitler's spell. It was almost as if there was no-one in there, just an empty shell to be filled with whatever a more powerful figure told him.

The man looked like a dog who had been smacked on the muzzle with a newspaper, and whose owner was about to strike a second blow. A cringing, whining, coward. Fleming knew the type, and loathed them.

"Well? Unable to talk without your mighty Führer here? Need his hand up your arse before you can open your mouth, do you?"

But at the mention of the Führer, Hess seemed to change almost into a different man. His spine straightened, and his expression grew more determined.

"Shit," Fleming thought, "that was exactly the wrong thing

to say."

Hess closed his eyes, and started humming a melody Fleming couldn't quite place, though it was one he knew he recognised from somewhere. Fleming tried speaking, and made a few feints as if to punch Hess, but the prisoner no longer acknowledged his existence. His mind was elsewhere, and he was no longer interested in communicating.

There was no point, Fleming realised after a few minutes, in even attempting to get the man to say a word. Nothing would open him up right now. In a few days, yes, he'd be willing to talk again, but right now Fleming would have to pursue other avenues of investigation.

He left the room, and the prisoner, whose humming continued until he was out of earshot.

Chapter 5

Ian Fleming hadn't had much of a chance to head into town recently. While he was technically still working at the Admiralty, he'd been seconded to Bletchley for several months now, and London was too far away, and too dangerous, for him to travel there casually. So when Dennis Wheatley invited him to come into the city for a drink, Fleming jumped at the excuse. Wheatley was one of the few people in the world that Fleming knew could both be trusted and be helpful with his problem.

Fleming and Wheatley had been friendly acquaintances for some time, and Fleming couldn't help but admire the older man. Wheatley had had few of Fleming's advantages in life, but had nonetheless managed to rise to a much higher station than Fleming had, thanks largely to the success of a series of novels he had written which combined espionage and international intrigue with plenty of sexualised violence. And Wheatley's new-found wealth had allowed him to live the kind of extravagant life to which Fleming could only aspire.

They met in Wheatley's club. It was one of the more discreet establishments, and one where rationing didn't seem to have affected the ability to get a decent meal and a good drink. Conversation during dinner was mostly casual – mutual acquaintances' latest romantic escapades, the sales of Wheatley's most recent book (a potboiling thriller about occult forces aiding the Nazis, which Fleming had made sure to read before the meeting), and the lamentably socialistic policies being pursued by the National Government in recent weeks.

After dining, they retired to leather armchairs, with a glass of Imperial Tokay for Wheatley, a whisky for Fleming, and Hoyo de Monterrey cigars, to discuss more serious matters. After a reasonable amount of small talk for appearances' sake, Wheatley set his glass down on the small table between them and turned to Fleming.

"This Hess business – your doing, I take it?"

"Now, Dennis, you know I couldn't possibly tell you that even if it were true, at least in a public place such as this."

"Nonsense. You know as well as I do that the men at this club are, without exception, as trustworthy as any in the Empire."

"Even so."

"Come now, you must have *something* you can tell me?"

"Not about Hess, directly, but something you may find interesting."

"Oh?"

"I'm planning to get in touch with Aleister Crowley soon. I have a little job of work for which he may be useful. Given the subject of your recent novels, I thought it might amuse you."

Wheatley raised an eyebrow. "You are joking, I hope?"

"What do you mean?"

"The man's an absolute monster. The very Devil himself."

"Then I shall be sure to bring my longest spoon. But you know Crowley, I believe?"

"A little, to my shame."

"Have you any advice?"

"Well, you've already refused my most important advice – to avoid him at all costs. But whatever you do, don't mispronounce his name like that. He has a little rhyme – his name is Crowley, because he is so holy, and his enemies call him Crowley, in wish to treat him foully."

"Noted."

"I know Crowley of old. He can be a charmer, if he wants to. Frightfully clever, frightfully witty. But *cold* with it. And the man's a bugger. Of course, you and I are men of the world, we know that such things go on. But he's *proud* of his beastliness."

"Many of them are. Goes with the territory."

Wheatley nodded and took a sip of his Imperial Tokay. "Crowley's an odd fish all round. Writes about sacrificing children, engages in the most frightful beastliness imaginable, and a cruel, cruel, bastard of a man. But he has his own principles, of a sort, and if you're on the level with him he might help you. But don't trust him an inch."

"I'll bear it in mind. Anything else I should know?"

Wheatley paused for a second, then drained his glass and placed it on the table. He leaned in, a serious look on his face.

"Look. I know you're a sceptic about this whole magic business. So am I. You know I'm a rational man. But... have you ever heard of a poet called Victor Neuberg?"

"Can't say I have. He any good?"

"No. But that's not the point. Crowley performed an enchantment on him and convinced him he'd been turned into a camel!"

"Had he?"

"No, of course not!"

"So what's the problem?"

"The problem is that, using only the power of his mind, Crowley managed to convince him that he had been. Poor man ended up in an asylum. Still there, as far as I know."

"Surely he could just have been doolally to start with?"

"Possibly, possibly. I mean, very few people spending time with Crowley are liable to have their heads completely screwed on, are they?"

Wheatley snapped his fingers in the air, and within seconds a waiter had brought refills of the two men's drinks. It was reassuring, Fleming thought to himself, that in these times of rationing and austerity it was still possible to live a civilised life in the capital, if one had the right friends.

"Still," Wheatley continued, "it's disturbing just how many people in Crowley's life end up dead, or mad, or both. He turns everyone against him eventually, because he cares nothing about anyone other than himself, and he's elevated his narcissism almost to the level of a religious principle. He's a very dangerous man."

Fleming sipped his drink and thought for a while, trying to find the best way of phrasing the next thought.

"Look, Dennis. . . I see two possibilities here. Either Crowley has no powers other than an ability to persuade the gullible to do what he wants – in which case we can make use of him, or. . ."

"Or?"

"Or Crowley *is* a magician, and magic does exist. In which case, given that the Germans have been looking into magic for years, we need to be able to make use of his magic, and quickly."

"And you think you can make use of a man like Crowley? Rather try to make use of a bull elephant in musk."

"Ah, but a bull elephant charging at one's enemies could be a great deal of use."

"Quite. Until the moment it turns around."

Fleming sipped his whisky thoughtfully, and the talk turned to other matters.

Chapter 6

In the tiny house in Torquay in which he resided, the Great Beast 666, To Mega Therion, Frater Perdurabo, or, as he was known to most of the population, Aleister Crowley, was making breakfast – a single boiled egg, toast, and a cup of tea. He told himself that his meditative practices would make this a sensory feast as great as any orgy, the texture of the yolk on his tongue as exquisite as the finest opium, but he still faced it with a weariness born of age.

Crowley had, in the past, been an imposing figure, a great hulk of a man whose bald head and piercing eyes could intimidate the most fearless of men into submission. He had been a mountaineer of the top rank, and a practising yogi who could bend his body into *asanas* which would have caused agony for even the most flexible of non-adepts. Now, though, he was sallow, his angular cheekbones showing through sagging skin. His head, no longer shaved, was fringed by tufts of white hair stained yellow by tobacco smoke. His digestion was permanently destroyed by his herculean intake of opiates, coca leaf, and absinthe. While he railed against the privations rationing caused him, he knew that in reality his diet would not be much different even were he to dine at the Savoy every evening. He never had been much good at self-deception, though that would never stop him trying.

He placed his egg-cup, toast-rack, butter dish, cup, saucer, and teapot on the tray with an exacting precision, then picked up the tray and shuffled over to his dining table. He placed the tray on the table, pulled out a chair, and sat down. He buttered his toast slowly, treating the rhythm of the knife strokes as a yogic mantra.

There was a pile of post on the table, which he had collected earlier. He opened the envelopes with his butter knife, and flicked through the letters desultorily. There were the usual missives from admirers; one from Lady Frieda Harris talking about the stultifying details of an undoubtedly tedious, but potentially lucrative, exhibition of her art, would need his attention at some point. He put it to one side and looked through the rest.

There was little of interest there. He sipped at his tea and winced to himself. There had been a time, not so long ago, when he would have disdained utterly a cup of tea made from what tasted like dust sweepings and mouse droppings, but that time had passed. This was his life now; soft-boiled eggs and flavourless grey liquids. He sighed and picked up the next letter.

Bills. Bills from the Gas Board, bills from the grocer, bills from all sides. And nothing to pay them with except a meagre income which came from public speaking and the decreasing sales of his books. Crowley could remember a time when he could have his books printed in tasteful, unique, editions for initiates only. Now, they were a commercial proposition to be sold like jars of mustard, and to an audience that could not even tell that they were being insulted in every word. And yet they still didn't sell enough.

He sliced his toast into soldiers, each strip as thin as possible in order to prolong the meal. He picked up one, dipped it in the egg yolk once, twice, three times, timing his breathing to match the dunks, and took a bite. At least the egg was good, even if the bread was the cheap, nasty, stuff that was all that could be obtained at present.

Let the yolk settle on the tongue. Feel the sticky, viscous, texture. Taste the sulphurous yellow liquid, and then let it slide down the throat along with the bread before the taste of the bread reaches the tongue. Maximise the pleasure, minimise the discomfort. Treat it as a yogic practice.

He continued looking through the letters. Quite a mountain of post he'd collected today — if not an Everest, then at least a... no, best not think of *that* particular mountain. Some things were best forgotten, and into that category he put most of his correspondence as well.

One letter, however, did have something of interest about it. It was from Naval Intelligence, addressed to "Mr. Aleister Crowley", and he thought about casting it aside then and there without reading further, given the British Government's stubborn refusal to use his proper title. He relented, though, and decided to show the usurper's lackeys the grace and magnanimity they so obviously refused him. He glanced through it, and saw they were asking for his assistance in the matter of Rudolf Hess.

He chuckled to himself. In the last war, half the press had been convinced he was a German spy, but now he was being asked to perform a similar task for the usurper's Government. How times had changed.

Only a few years ago, the same newspapers that had called him "the wickedest man in England" had been printing headlines like "Hurrah for the Blackshirts!" and praising Herr Hitler's wise governance. He wondered if, should the German invasion succeed, Rothermere's papers would once again become the arse-licking lackeys of the German Führer. He suspected so.

Crowley had no great love for the Government headed by the supposed King, and the chaos and disruption caused by war were distractions from his meditative practices. He composed his reply bearing these factors, and others, in mind:

> Sir,
>
> If it is true that Herr Hess is much influenced by astrology and Magick, my services might be of use

to the Department, in case he should not be willing to do what you wish.

Col. J. F. C. Carter ..., Thomas N. Driberg ..., Karl J. Germer ..., could testify to my status and reputation in these matters.

I have the honour to be, Sir,

Your obedient servant Aleister Crowley.

After writing his response, he carefully burned the letter he had received, while chanting under his breath, before heading off to the post office.

Chapter 7

In his office at Bletchley, Turing sipped on his tea, and winced. Rationing was making even the smallest pleasures of life almost intolerable. Between the small quantities of poor-quality tea, the measly portion of milk the ration board allowed, and the total unavailability of lemons, it was becoming almost impossible to make a drinkable cup.

He stared at it, half wondering if someone had replaced his drink with old dishwater. Certainly the colour and taste were similar – the greyish liquid in the cup bore little resemblance to anything he would have thought of as tea before the war – but there was a metallic greasiness to it that could only come from a military institutional tea urn. No, this was his tea all right, more's the pity.

There was nothing for it. He would have to drink the foul muck. He needed the refreshment in order to get to work, and he was working on what seemed to be an insoluble problem. He took a large gulp – better to get it over with. There was nothing to savour in that cup.

He remembered how tea had once been an actual pleasure. One of the few in which a man could indulge without guilt, without worry for his health, and without even the risk of disgrace or imprisonment. Tea, mathematics, and running, and little else, had made life worth living. Now he had no time for running, and the tea was undrinkable. But at least he had an actual intellectual problem to sink his teeth into again.

He looked again at the documents he'd been given. The fact that they had been brought into the country by Hess was, of course, important, but more important from Turing's perspective was the fact that these documents were not a standard German cipher. None of them made any sense at all, and without some kind of crib or idea of what was in them, it was useless to even try decrypting them — but that was precisely why they were such an interesting challenge; the first really good one Turing had had in months.

"I've tried a few techniques — basic frequency analysis, that sort of thing — in case it's a simple substitution cipher or something of the sort. It isn't, but it may be as simple as two plaintexts summed together. When I try these things, I get little fragments of sense, but it quickly turns into gibberish again."

He knew he had to stop talking to himself — walls had ears, and careless talk cost lives, and all the other homilies that were included on the garish coloured posters plastered over every vertical surface everywhere one looked these days — but it was a habit that was hard to break, and sometimes one needed an intelligent conversation.

It definitely wasn't the Enigma code, that much he knew. They'd broken the codes for every day up to Hess' arrival, and every day since for that matter. It didn't match any of them. Anyway, they wouldn't have allowed an Enigma to be brought into the country. Too dangerous. It had to be some sort of pen-and-paper cipher.

But what? It didn't seem likely to be a one-time pad — as far as he knew, the Germans never used them. Too risky, when they had a crypto system they could use instead, and which as far as the Germans knew was unbreakable. But if it wasn't Enigma, or any of the lesser systems they used, that seemed to leave only some system that only Hess himself knew. And of course, Hess wasn't talking.

Turing knew that the solution must be obvious — pen-and-paper codes had not really advanced much since the time of

Julius Caesar, and any schoolboy could, with sufficient ingenuity, break one. The problem was that "sufficient ingenuity"
could in this case mean days or weeks of work, and if the information was about some new German battle-plan, he may not
have the time.

Was it keyed to some book? If so, it would have to be one
easily available in Britain, and in an edition to which Hess had
had access while still in Germany.

He looked again at the sheets. He'd made clean, typewrit-
ten, copies of the documents, which had originally been in Hess'
almost-unreadable handwriting. He had, of course, first made
sure that there was nothing about the documents themselves
that may be of use, but there was no sign of any steganographic
system being used. No letters were out of place, no unusual
spacing, no pin-pricks above important letters. Just page after
page of gibberish.

He finished the drink, and chained his mug back to the
radiator, pocketing the key once again. Ridiculous that in a top-
security environment, where decisions that would affect the fate
of the nation were made and where everyone was trusted to keep
secrets which, if revealed, could lead to the very destruction of
the Empire itself, he had to keep his tea mug chained up in
case of theft.

It just went to show, he supposed, that people's behaviour
in the public and private spheres was different, as if people wore
different masks for different occasions, and it was impossible to
judge what, if anything, was happening in the brains behind
those masks.

But at least with people you had clues – not just their words,
but their tone of voice, their body language, their facial expressions. You could watch and listen to those clues, and with
enough work you could figure out what was going on inside
their heads. You'd never be able to decrypt it perfectly, of
course – there simply wasn't enough data leakage for that –
but you could get a good enough idea. You had something to

go on.

But if one could work out people's motives from their actions, surely it must be possible to work out the much simpler
puzzle of what Hess' text contained, given the much larger
amount of data available? Looked at that way, the task before
him was almost trivial. He could do it. He knew he could.

He got back to work.

Chapter 8

Even during a war unlike any that had been seen in the history of the world, the business of government still had to continue, and in Britain part of that business is allowing the hereditary aristocracy a space in the legislature in which to voice their opinions on every topic known to humanity.

There are countries in the world in which the voice of the people is paramount – *vox populi, vox dei* – while in other countries it is the voice of a single leader that must not be countermanded in any circumstances. For the British Empire, though, the voices of those who were bred for privilege and power, and the leaders of the Established Church, had veto power over all others. Continuity, and the establishment, were all.

Britain's legislature had, for centuries, been split into two houses. The lower house, the House of Commons, was, as the name suggested, made up of common people. Or at least, people who hadn't yet risen to the first rank of the nobility – the members of Parliament had very few coal miners or street sweepers among their ranks, and rather a lot of men with knighthoods.

The House of Lords, on the other hand, was for the uncommon – the hereditary aristocracy, the newly ennobled, and the Bishops.

The same night that Hess had made his flight, the Palace of Westminster, in which both houses of Parliament sat, had been bombed by the Germans. Parliament had lost its ancient home, and both houses were currently relegated to the church annexe of the Palace. But the change of venue did not mean that the ancient role of the Lords had changed.

Since before Parliament had a home at all, the nobility had had its say in the affairs of state. They represented continuity – their families had owned England, and later the United Kingdom, for centuries, and they intended to keep it that way. Elected politicians could come and go every few years and change their views with the prevailing winds, but there would always be a Duke of Westminster, and he would always have the same interests as his grandfather had and his grandson would.

Of course, some things had changed over the years. Many of the older peers were still nostalgic for the days before Lloyd George had filled the place up with boot-polish merchants and jumped-up tobacconists, who had bought their way to an Earldom. And even more so, they were nostalgic for the time before the other great change that the Liberals had made to their privileges, introducing the Parliament Act and making it clear in law that the House of Commons, not the Lords, had primacy when it came to legislation.

Nonetheless, the Lords still had their place, and still represented Britain's traditions. They were there to advise the monarch, and to ensure the Government had regard to events further away than the next election.

And so, as they had since the days of Simon de Montfort, the Lords Temporal and Spiritual were assembled in Parliament, and were making their views known to a public that hung on their every word, at least as far as they were aware. Their words were duly recorded by the few reporters given access to Parliament during the War, and then largely unprinted in favour of the events of the day. But this lack of public interest did not concern them, any more than the fact that the Prime Minister was largely ignoring them and governing according to his own sense of military strategy.

The Lord who was, at the present moment, voicing his opinions was Lord Keynsham, a short, podgy man, with a shock of white hair that looked as if someone had stuck a mop on top of his head. The subject of the great man's speech to the nation was the threat of Satanist-controlled Communists taking over the country, and in particular the threat caused by Tom Driberg, the *Daily Express'* "William Hickey" columnist.

"Hitler is a distraction, mark my words. Man needs to be put down like a rabid dog, of course, no question of that – no-one can be allowed to attack the British Empire and get away with it, still less to have this place and the other place bombed. Damned impertinence of the man! – but we mustn't let him take our minds off the Reds. Hitler is a man. Stalin is controlled by Satan himself. The very Devil. Mark my words."

Driberg, sat in the gallery, laughed to himself. Keynsham was a relic, like one of Wodehouse's more pompous Earls or Dukes. Driberg was more of an Evelyn Waugh man himself, and saw Keynsham as one more symbol of the decline and fall of the British Empire.

Even had Driberg been a spy for the Russians – and had Keynsham had as much access to the secret world of espionage as he pretended, he would have known that in fact Driberg was spying *on* the Russians – he would not have been worried by Keynsham's rambling threats. The poor man was deluded.

While Keynsham liked to pretend he was a great aristocrat, everyone with any real knowledge knew his father was a brewer who'd bought a peerage from Lloyd George thirty years earlier, and promptly dropped dead, leaving his idiot son with the title. Driberg liked to remind him of that in his column, to Keynsham's evident ire.

"And the worst fifth columnist in this country – the one who, more than any of the Mosleyites, is doing his bit to destroy morale and weaken our great nation – is William Hickey of the *Daily Express*. The evil of his words is all the greater for their apparent patriotism. This is a man who pretends to support the war effort, and who pretends to support Britain, but who through drips of insinuation is slowly wearing down the public morale. Mark my words. Mark them, I say. William Hickey is the man who will bring about the destruction of the British Empire."

Driberg started to realise that Keynsham actually didn't know that William Hickey was merely a pseudonym. This could be interesting. . . if Keynsham was genuinely unaware of his identity, then Driberg might be able to make use of him. This would require some serious thought. . .

Chapter 9

Before the war, travelling to Torquay had mostly been for pleasure – holidaymakers would travel down to the south west to swim in the town's famously blue waters, to marvel at the sights, and to look out over the ocean. Now, however, the journey was made most often by evacuees, desperate to get away from the danger of London.

The south west of England had always, though, been a place unto itself, with different mores, a different accent, and a different, slower, pace of life than the metropolis. Ian Fleming had once heard someone talk about how the difference between Britain and America was that in America a hundred years was a long time, while in Britain a hundred miles was a long way. The hundred-and-sixty or so miles between London and Torquay seemed an almost insurmountable distance culturally, if not geographically.

This was not a place of clubs and chaps who knew chaps. This was a place where everyone knew everyone, and where strangers were not welcome, even though the town had built itself on tourism. People from out of town were perfectly fine to spend their money on overpriced ices and watered beer, but they were not to be talked to, or to be treated as people rather than walking wallets.

And because of this reticence, and a general reluctance to give directions, Fleming had some difficulty finding his target, and it was almost dark before he arrived. Aleister Crowley had apparently moved relatively recently, and Fleming found him not in a Gothic mansion or abandoned monastery, but in a small, white-painted, suburban house.

Fleming's knock had been answered by a frail-looking old man, who bore such little resemblance to the Great Beast of legend that Fleming had needed to make sure he'd come to the right place.

"I'm looking for Aleister Crowley".

"Do what thou wilt shall be the whole of the law," said the skinny, balding old man, with the white goatee, with bits of egg-yolk in his beard.

"An interesting creed. But not, perhaps, a useful one during a war."

"Come through to my dining room, and we might discuss its utility in comfort."

Crowley led Fleming through to a small dining room, whose window opened onto a view of the green fields nearby. He sat at the single chair pulled up to a round wooden coffee table, on which was a cup of tea, much of which seemed to have spilled into the saucer on which the cup was placed, and an eggcup containing a half-eaten boiled egg with a spoon still inside it.

Crowley gestured to the one other chair in the room, and Fleming pulled it up to the table.

"Do sit down," Crowley said, after Fleming had taken his seat. He picked up his spoon, and finished off his egg, eating slowly and methodically, and dabbing his mouth with a napkin after every bite. Only when he had finished eating did he resume the conversation. "Now, you believe that doing one's will is an anarchist creed. Far from it. Should the policemen and judges of this world be let loose on society, it would be a veritable hell. One cannot do one's will until one understands what that will is, and very few people have attained such a level of understanding."

Crowley smiled, a gentle smile which quite surprised Fleming with his charm. Crowley had an imposing reputation, but the elderly gentleman here did indeed seem a gentle man. There was a kindness to him which quite belied Wheatley's fearsome warnings. Fleming decided he was going to like this man.

Crowley dabbed his mouth again with his napkin, smearing the egg yolk without managing to remove any of it, then continued talking.

"Anyway, I do not normally enter into metaphysical debate until I have been introduced to my interlocutor. You would be?"

"My name is Ian Fleming, sir, and I have come on behalf of Naval Intelligence."

"Ah, so you would be here about the Hess affair. Most perplexing. Why would an intelligent man think that Britain would – now, of all times – be interested in surrender? A year ago, maybe. But we have struggled through enough, and lost enough, that to back down without victory would be a betrayal of the dead."

"Indeed. I'm sure he has his reasons, though."

"Oh, I wouldn't be at all surprised if you knew what those reasons were. But you in the intelligence services know more than most the wisdom of the command to know, to dare, to will, and to keep silence. I shall not press you on matters which are beyond the scope of my activities, and shall assume that you will inform me of any matters which are germane."

Crowley reached into his jacket pocket and took out a small, zippered, pouch. He opened it, and nestled in what looked like a velvet lining was a syringe.

"I hope you don't mind, sir, if I take my regular infusion of diamorphine?"

Fleming nodded his assent, and Crowley tied off his left arm, found a vein, and injected the fluid. His expression immediately changed into one of vacant bliss – rather more quickly, Fleming thought, than the drug could have affected him; Fleming wondered if this was all an act, and if Crowley had injected some inert substance rather than the narcotic.

The two men talked for some time about trivial matters, and Fleming noted that Crowley's train of thought seemed to drift, more or less at random. He would be talking about the insignia of the Nazis, and then suddenly break off and start talking about the Egyptian god Noor-Ra-Huit, or he would ask about Hess and, before Fleming had a chance to answer, would go on into a digression about demonic possession.

Eventually, Fleming managed to steer the topic around to the purpose of his visit.

"So, Mr. Crowley, what help, precisely, do you think you can provide His Majesty's Government in the matter of Herr Hess?"

"Oh, I thought maybe I could perform an exorcism on him. Or maybe telepathically contact him and extract the appropriate information from him."

Fleming paused before replying. "You're offering. . . to perform a magic spell? That's your offer?"

"Indeed. I shall magickally extract any information you require from his skull."

"We were rather hoping that you should, perhaps, merely intimidate him. Put on a show of some sort, or offer him occult secrets in return for his co-operation."

"My dear sir!" Crowley's expression was a perfect mask of offence, save for his eyes, which were glittering. "You ask me to perform. . . fakery? To prostitute my life's work?"

"I apologise if I have caused any offence. But you must understand that His Majesty's Government does not believe that telepathic powers have any effect. Your magic can't be of any use to us."

Crowley rose.

"In that case, sir, I fear we have nothing further to discuss. Please give my regards to Mr. Wheatley."

Fleming was half-way down the street before he realised that he had not mentioned Wheatley to Crowley at all.

Chapter 10

Section B5(B) of the Security Service had a very different remit from the rest of MI5. While most of the service was devoted to fairly routine espionage operations, Section B5(B) operated out of separate offices, and had little contact with the rest of the service. It had to keep secrets even from the rest of the organisation, because its job was to infiltrate subversive movements, and to report back on their activities. Only one man, known as "M", knew everything that his section was up to, and he kept it to himself. Fleming and Turing had made arrangements to meet up with him, to make sure that their plans weren't going to involve them treading on his toes.

Maxwell Knight was someone Fleming had known for some time, but had never really been able to understand. The man was a mystery wrapped inside an enigma wrapped inside a bully who could destroy an underling with a well-chosen expletive, and nobody Fleming knew had ever got close enough to him to understand what made him tick.

His office gave little indication of his importance. It was functional – a desk, filing cabinets, a telephone, and little else. There were windows, but they were kept closed and blinded at all times, and the light in the room came from a desk lamp. Like much about the Security Service, the office gave away little about what activities took place there, and even less about the character of the man who did the work.

While the rooms through which they had walked had been

full of the noise of ringing telephones and clattering typewriters, Knight's office was sufficiently insulated that the only sound in the room was of its occupant scratching away with his pen at the papers he was reviewing.

Fleming was always slightly intimidated when he entered Knight's office, but Turing seemed utterly oblivious to the importance of the man they were visiting – either that, or his casual stance was the product of a better actor than Fleming thought him.

While Fleming was stood firmly erect, Turing was slouched over, scratching at his ear distractedly, and humming under his breath. Fleming nudged him with his elbow, and the noise stopped for approximately thirty seconds, then started again.

They waited for a while while Knight, apparently unaware of their presence, continued to work through the papers on his desk. Eventually, Fleming gave a slight cough and spoke.

"Major Knight."

"Ian. And who's this with you?"

"This is Alan Turing, one of the boffins we're working with up at Bletchley. Quite a remarkable mind."

"Really? Not got much time for the remarkable myself. It's the normal we need. A remarkable spy would be no use, would he?"

"Indeed," Turing replied, although Knight had not yet addressed him, "but not everyone is a spy. And while the normal people do have their part to play, so do the remarkable. The world needs all kinds of people, Sir Maxwell. It's the Hitlers of this world who want everyone to be the same – it's not a very British attitude, is it?"

Knight gave a slight "hmph", and appeared to decide that Turing was a lost cause. He turned his attention back to Fleming.

"So, what are you after, man?"

"Well, Sir Maxwell, I'd like you to give me the latest on what's been going on with Hess. I've been away for a couple of days, and I'm sure any information would be useful to Turing."

"And what's Turing doing, that he needs the information?"

"He's the one who's trying to decrypt the documents."

"Ah. I see... and where exactly have you been, anyway?"

"It's rather embarrassing, sir. I'm afraid it was a bit of a wild goose chase. I went to visit Aleister Crowley, in the mistaken belief that he might be of some use to us."

"Aleister!" Knight's eyebrows shot up, "Good God! How is the old rogue?"

"You know him, sir?"

"Oh, yes. I studied with him back in the thirties. Far, far cleverer man than you might think. Knows his stuff, all right."

"So you know him well then?"

"Oh yes. Introduced him to your friend Wheatley, too. Wheatley only saw him a handful of times, though I believe they corresponded a little afterwards. For myself... well, the man's definitely a cad, no question of that. But he's a cad who knows what he's about. Plays his cards close to his chest."

"So you think there may be something to his Satan-worshipping?"

"Oh, he's no Satanist. His beliefs are far more idiosyncratic than that. He has invented his own religion, with elements of every mad belief that has crossed his path and taken his fancy, but Satan isn't a part of it."

"Really?"

"Oh yes. What Crowley believes is that he is himself a god, but that anyone can attain that rank. 'Every man and every woman is a star', he says. The idea is that we're in a new age, the aeon of Thelema as he calls it. He claims he was given a revelation by the Egyptian gods."

"Surely no-one can believe in the Egyptian gods in this day and age? This is the twentieth century!"

"Indeed it is. But Crowley believes that those gods are still there, and that we are in the early days of a new religion – one of which he is the founder, prophet, and thus far only real believer."

Turing interrupted "Sorry to butt in here, but is all this really relevant to the matter at hand?"

Knight grinned. "Ah, you're one of *that* type, are you? Man who knows the value of everything and the price of nothing? Well, we'll get down to business then, shall we?"

Fleming nodded. Knight was, despite his apparent impatience, clearly starting to respect Turing, as he had expected he would.

Knight continued, "There's really not much news to give you. Hess has been transferred to the Tower, but he's still not talking. But Ian, you might want to have a word with Tom Driberg. He may be able to help you. . ."

Chapter 11

The Queen's House at the Tower of London is one of the most remarkable surviving pieces of British architectural history – a building that was meant for the protection and comfort of the most respected traitors, for their relaxation before their execution. It was created as a very British compromise, much as they wrapped the noose in leather so the hangman didn't hurt the victim's poor, delicate neck.

The most recent guest to be held at the Queen's House was not a traitor as such – or if he was, it was not to Britain, but to his own country. Rudolf Hess had been held there for several days now, in the hope that the pleasant environment might persuade him to open up, and to be more willing to discuss his mission. So far, though, that hadn't happened – he had been happy to talk about many subjects, but not about why he had come to Britain.

When Ian Fleming entered Hess'...cell hardly seemed the right word any more, though "quarters" also didn't have the right ring to it...the difference from the cell in which their previous meeting had taken place could not have been greater. Yes, there were still bars on the windows and guards on the door, but the room in which he found Hess was spacious, bright, and airy, with nothing of the stench that had permeated the earlier cell.

Fleming thought that putting Hess in such a place was a mistake, for several reasons, not least of which was that he believed that Hess would see it as a reward for his lack of co-operation. He was surprised, though, to see that in his new surroundings Hess was much friendlier, greeting Fleming with a smile and an extended hand, neither of which were reciprocated.

"Prisoner Hess."

"Commander Fleming."

"I trust your new surroundings are to your taste?"

"An interesting place this, you know? The guards told me it is called the Queen's House because here is where Anne Boleyn stayed before her marriage to one of your kings. And she stayed here again, just before they chopped her head off. Is that what you plan to do to me, when you have what you need from me? A quick axe through the neck?"

"Guy Fawkes also stayed here."

"I do not know who he is, I am afraid."

"A traitor. He was executed, too. He was hanged, drawn, and quartered. That's when they hang you until you're almost dead, cut you down, chop off your privates and burn them in front of your eyes, pull out your innards, and then cut you up into four pieces."

"I see. "

"Do you think that would be appropriate for you?"

"I am no traitor."

"Hitler says you are."

"The Führer sometimes has to say things he does not mean. If my mission fails, he has to disown me."

"Your mission already has failed."

"We shall see."

"We have your documents. You are not going to see Hamilton."

"That may well be the case. Or it may be that you change your mind. I am prepared to take that chance – after all, what other choice do I have? If I talk to you, my mission has definitely failed. If I don't, well, there may still be a chance for success."

Fleming smiled. The prisoner was nowhere near as cautious as he thought. He was keeping the purpose of his visit to himself, but was leaking information all the time. Merely by seeing what he was saying and which subjects he was avoiding, it was possible to form an idea of his intentions.

"Oh, there is absolutely no chance of success. You have said that you flew here to negotiate a peace. Yet you refuse to negotiate, and your Führer disowns you. All you have to look forward to, now, for the rest of your life, is prison, and the knowledge that you have failed at the most important task you ever set yourself."

"Not if the Reich wins."

"They won't. We both know it."

"Nevertheless."

"Well, if the Nazis win, you'll end up in a concentration camp, instead of a prison, for betraying Hitler. Not much of an improvement, I'd say."

"I have not betrayed the Führer."

"He says you have."

Hess' face was starting to redden, and his heavy eyebrows, always his most prominent feature, furrowed, instantly ageing him by almost a decade. His voice cracked as he replied. "I have *not* betrayed the Führer, and he knows this as well as anyone."

"So you're calling Hitler a liar, are you?"

Hess' voice was now noticeably higher than it had been earlier, and he sounded as if his throat was pinched, even though he was clearly attempting to appear calm. "He is no liar. He sometimes has to say things he does not mean. The propaganda, you know?"

"Maybe. Or maybe he means it. Maybe he thinks you've failed him. He says you're to be executed if the Nazis get their hands on you, you know."

"As I say, he has to say things he does not mean."

Fleming smiled. "Remember Ernst Röhm? Did he think he had betrayed Hitler? Or did he think he was loyal to the last?

Your Führer doesn't treat his former friends very well."

At this, Hess' voice became much louder, and Fleming could see his shoulders straighten, as if readying to attack. "I am *nothing* like Röhm. That subhuman degenerate was a...no, I shall not even say the word. I have never...never..."

"Really? Not even when you were in prison with your Führer? Surrounded only by other men, spending all day with the man you admire most? All men get urges, you know."

Hess was by this point trembling with a barely suppressed fury.

"You dare? You *dare* say these things? Have you no decency?"

Fleming laughed. "You of all people should know better than to talk about decency. What's decent about the Nazis?"

He waited, but Hess didn't reply, merely standing in place, trembling, breath coming out of his nose in audible snorts.

"Oh well," Fleming looked at his watch. "I can't stand here all day chatting. Some of us have places to be. Do let me know if you decide you want to talk."

Fleming was almost out of earshot before he heard the scream of rage coming from Hess' cell. One more visit and Hess would crack, he knew it.

Chapter 12

Turing had cracked the code. It had been simple enough in the end, and he'd been surprised it had taken him so long – it had ended up being a minor piece of number crunching. Hess had not used a one-time pad, but had instead summed his plaintext with a known piece of text – which had turned out to be the first few pages of *Mein Kampf*. Hess clearly knew nothing of cryptanalysis, or he'd have realised how easy it would be to break such a code, even without knowing the key. It had only taken Turing so long because he'd assumed that the deputy Führer would have had access to some of the Reich's more powerful techniques, and had headed down a few dead ends as a result.

In future, he would remember not to assume complexity. If one technique takes half an hour, and another takes a week, try the half-hour one first even if it seems much less likely to succeed.

After breaking the code, it almost seemed anticlimactic to read the actual text. It appeared to be a description of rituals to be carried out at dawn on the summer solstice. But what those rituals could be for, Turing didn't know – except that given the source, they were unlikely to be anything good.

"At midnight, at the start of the longest day of the year, gather and perform these tasks. Before the time of the golden dawn, and the new sunrise, there must be darkness and death. Drink the elixir and prepare, for when the dawn comes you will see with new eyes the cleansing light of the truth."

He read through the document carefully, sipping his foul-tasting tea as he did, but not really noticing the taste. It was absolutely fascinating for someone who, like Turing, had little time for occultists of any stripe. How could people believe this absolute rot? It made no sense at all to him.

He crossed his legs, stuck his finger between the grey, woollen, sock he was wearing and his leg, and scratched at his ankle. Damnable wartime shortages meant that there was no such thing as a comfortable pair of socks to be had any more, and his feet were constantly distracting him with their itching.

He turned his mind back to the paper in front of him. Much of it was fairly innocent – dancing and celebrating the dawn. Harmless fun, more like Morris dancing than anything. But then suddenly in the last couple of lines, it started to talk about "the sacrifice of the perfect victim".

Turing had flicked through Frazer at university, and knew what that meant. But surely midsummer was the wrong time of year for that sort of thing? Normally you'd do that in midwinter, to try to bring the sun back. The longest day of the year made no sense for a ceremony to bring back the light . . .

And a single word at the end – Barbarossa.

The whole thing had a curious flow to it. For all that the ceremony's purpose remained opaque, there was a fascinating logic to it. He could see how every point of the ceremony led, logically and inevitably, to the next point. What it meant, he didn't know, but there were patterns there.

Turing's whole training, first as a mathematician and later as a cryptographer, had been designed to make him able to see patterns wherever they existed, and he did worry at times that it also led him to see patterns that weren't really there. But this time, it was too obvious. There really was something to his intuition here.

He ran his hands through his hair, distractedly. There was a hidden pattern here below the surface. It was almost like steganography – disguising a message in a larger one, full of irrelevant noise. Unless you knew exactly which bits to pick out, it would just look like a pointless pagan ritual.

He looked through the text more carefully, trying to pick out which elements were meaningless and which meaningful. The first task was just to cut out all the waffle about cleansing lights and truth and gold. Break it down into a series of steps, like an algorithm. A mechanical task that could be performed without thought. At *this* time, take *this* implement, and wave it three times. At *this* time, say *these* words. And at the moment of dawn itself, slice the knife through the throat of the sacrificial victim.

Yes. Well.

Obviously this was nothing good – but he'd known that, already. The Nazis were hardly going to be sending Hess over with a recipe for Christmas cake, were they? The question wasn't what repulsive methods were described in the ritual, but what the end result of it would be.

Of course, the end result would be nothing – to say otherwise would be to admit the possibility of magic – but there must be an *intention*, a *purpose*. Those Turing would find. He knew it.

He pulled out a pencil and paper and started drawing diagrams. The participants in the ritual were acting almost like the components of a machine. The chanting... that had a timing element to it, didn't it? It was acting like a clock, to keep the ritualists in step. If *these* two were raising their arms at the same time, why three syllables later was *this* one dropping a sprig of mistletoe to the ground? (And where the hell were they going to get the mistletoe anyway, in the middle of summer?)

It was just a matter of encryption again. The creator of this ritual had wanted to accomplish a goal. He had encoded his intention in the steps of the ritual. Now all Turing had to do was work back the other way. What did those steps tell him about the psychology of the person behind it?

This was a message, but it wasn't saying what its sender thought. Somewhere encoded in this ritual was information about the eventual aims of the Nazis in the war. Given its origin, the information this magic spell contained about the psychology of the Nazi high command could be invaluable, even if the ritual itself was an obvious nonsense.

What was the sacrifice in aid of? That was the question, and Turing had to find the answer.

Chapter 13

Ian Fleming had been planning for a while to introduce Turing and Wheatley. While the two men were, in his opinion, unlikely to get along, they also both had inquisitive, fast-moving minds, of the kind that in Fleming's view was needed to get the most out of the work the intelligence services were doing. If they didn't end up murdering each other, they'd spark enough ideas between them to shorten the war by a year, if only a decent pretext could be found for bringing them together.

The opportunity had finally presented itself. Now Turing realised that the documents involved the occult, Wheatley's area of expertise, he'd been positively eager to meet the man, and had travelled down to London with Fleming, to meet at Wheatley's club as his guest.

Turing looked completely out of place in the confines of a luxurious gentlemen's club, and seemed almost to be twitching. Fleming knew that Turing had met with far more important people than Wheatley, even the Prime Minister himself, but it didn't seem to be the people as much as the objects that were setting him on edge. Turing just didn't fit in in an opulent background, and it showed on his face.

Wheatley was sitting at his usual table, and gave a faint nod to the two men as they approached.

"Dennis Wheatley, this is Alan Turing. Alan, this is Dennis."

Ever since the idea of the two men working together had first been mooted, Fleming had been very interested to see how they would react to each other. Sadly for him, they barely acknowledged each other, Turing merely reciprocating Wheatley's nod. Wheatley gestured to the chairs nearby, and Fleming and Turing sat down.

"So Alan, I believe you have some questions to ask Dennis."

"I do. I don't know how helpful he will be, but... Mr. Wheatley, do you actually have much knowledge of the world of the occult, or is the research for your books less accurate than it appears?"

Wheatley thought for a second. "That's a difficult question to answer. I have little first-hand, practical, experience, but I have spent enough time with those who have that I have a much better understanding than most laymen."

"I would like, if I may, to ask you to have a look over some documents for me. Now, understand that these are top secret – Mr. Wheatley does have the appropriate classification, doesn't he, Ian?"

Fleming nodded.

"That's a relief. Now, may I take it that you will treat these documents with the utmost secrecy."

Wheatley nodded, the ghost of a smirk appearing although he tried to hide it. "You may."

Turing passed the papers across, and Wheatley spent a few minutes examining them in what Turing thought was an excessive amount of detail.

Finally, Wheatley put the papers down, and looked thoughtfully at Turing.

"Young man, you asked me if I would treat these documents with the utmost secrecy. Now I must ask you something similar. In order to explain them to you, I shall have to reveal to you secrets which, should they enter into the wrong hands, could do the most frightful damage."

"You can trust me not to reveal anything you say to anyone, Mr. Wheatley."

Wheatley nodded. "I believe I can. But it's not simply

a matter of trust. I have sworn oaths, as part of initiation ceremonies, and consider those oaths to be sacred bonds with very real consequences. I have also, however, sworn an even more sacred oath, of loyalty to His Majesty the King, his heirs and successors. That higher oath does, I believe, allow me to give you the information, but only if I am certain that you are bound by equally strong oaths."

"Mr. Wheatley, I promise you, I am an honest man. I give you my word, and I consider that word to be at least as strong as any oath it is possible you have sworn. I cannot swear on anything but the truth, but I swear on that, and hope that is enough."

Wheatley nodded. "I see. Yes, yes I think that will do."

He put down the papers, and leaned back in his chair, as if to tell a long story.

"This ritual," he began, "is intended to revive England, and bring her back to a supposed past glory."

Turing interrupted. "But this is from the Nazis! Why would they want to revive Britain?"

Wheatley smiled. "Note that I said England, not Britain. That's one of the important points here. This ritual would, if carried out, bring about the revival of a very real spirit, that of the Saxon people who inhabited England before the Norman conquest. As a Germanic people, the Nazis believe that the Saxons would ally with them. They want to conjure up the spirit of the English people – not the Norman aristocracy, and not the Scots or the other Celts, but the old, pure-blooded, Anglo Saxons. They think that something in the English people will resist rule by the Norman French. A demon encouraging a treasonous uprising against the ruling classes, in the name of freedom."

"But isn't it the ruling classes themselves who are doing this? And aren't they rather against freedom?"

"Oh, Hitlerism is just a route to a greater anarchy at the end. And Crowley and his ilk believe that they will naturally rise to the top, once freed from the shackles of law and society. Filth."

"So this ritual is merely intended to conjure up a ghost?" Fleming asked.

"Oh, it's more than that. This ritual would, if carried out, destroy the British Empire."

"Destroy the Empire? Nonsense! The British Empire is the greatest the world has ever seen! She's at the height of her powers. How could a simple magic trick destroy that?"

"Empires do fall, Ian," replied Turing. "I'm not saying that this makes any sense, but empires do all fall, eventually."

Fleming turned purple.

"The Empires of the past fell because they became decadent, because they became weak, and allowed subversives to undermine them from within. That is not the case for the British Empire, and never will be!"

Turing nodded. "You may well be right. Of course I hope so."

Noting the tension between them, Wheatley took a calmer tone. "Of course the Empire is as strong as she ever was. We all know that. The question is whether Herr Hitler does. We have already seen that he has quite an outsize opinion of Germany's importance on the world stage. It is not difficult to imagine that he has an equally inaccurate opinion of Britain's unimportance."

Fleming nodded. "All right. I can see that."

"Let me have a think about how to proceed with this, Ian. Meet me back here in a week, and by then I should have the beginnings of a plan."

Chapter 14

The drive back towards Bletchley was, for the most part, a quiet one. Turing and Fleming sat in silence, watching the world go by and thinking about the conversation they'd just had, and about its implications for their own work.

Most of the time, the only sound other than the engine was Turing drumming his fingers on his trousers, and occasionally humming to himself. Fleming had driven this route enough times that the distraction wasn't too annoying, and so he let his companion think without asking him to contain himself. Experience had shown that Turing's eccentricities often led to brilliant insights.

After half an hour had passed, Turing finally spoke up.

"You don't really believe all this tosh about magic do you?"

"Of course not. But it doesn't matter if *we* believe it. What matters is that the Nazis do. They're a bunch of superstitious cowards, and we can use that against them."

"But Wheatley does?"

"Oh yes. He's one of those freethinkers who will believe in literally anything *except* Christianity. He has a violent aversion to the Church – particularly the Anglican Church – but he will believe in the Pagan gods, the life-force of Bernard Shaw, evolution, the power of Satan, magic, spiritualism...you name it, and he'll believe it. Some of it even with good reason."

"What do you mean, good reason?"

"Oh, Wheatley's got a very sharp mind under the hail-fellow-well-met stuff and the bluster. Any individual opinion he has is as likely to be rot as anything – he picks up opinions from everything from the *Daily Mail* to the *Gem* and *Magnet*, and doesn't really discriminate between them as far as I can see. But if you only listen to him when he's talking about his own experiences, rather than something he's read somewhere...well, he's a *lot* more interesting then."

"I see. So you think there's something to what he says?"

"Oh, no. Well, probably not. Again, he's picked up most of this from Charles Fort and from the rot Crowley talks, rather than from anything that's happened to him. But I wouldn't completely dismiss it. He's not a stupid man, and he may well know more than he's saying."

The drive continued in silence for a while, until Fleming suddenly said "Of course, you realise that we have to pass the documents on to their intended recipients?"

Turing looked over to Fleming as if the older man had gone mad. "I beg your pardon?"

"We need to give the documents to the people Hess was trying to get them to."

"I'm sorry, I must seem very dense, but are you seriously suggesting that we give top secret Nazi documents to fifth columnists?"

"I'm suggesting exactly that."

"Why?"

"Well, look at it this way. The documents themselves just describe a magical ritual, which we know won't work. With me so far?"

"Yes."

"The ritual can't possibly do any real harm. But it could be used to smoke the Link out. The reason Hess fell for the story about a group of Nazi-sympathising occultists in the aristocracy is that such people probably do exist. Not in any great number, and they're certainly not as powerful as we convinced Hess they were, but there are some out there, and we should do our best to track them down."

"You're joking?"

"I'm afraid not. Not everyone in the aristocracy has Britain's best interests at heart, I'm afraid. Many of them are cosmopolitan types, world travellers who don't see Britain as their home. They feel far closer to Berlin than to Barking or Dagenham, and have no great loyalty to the British people."

"But surely that kind of cosmopolitan would loathe everything the Nazis stand for?"

"Oh, I don't see why. Hitler is apparently a very charming man, according to those who have spent time in his presence. German culture is very easy to admire, and one can understand wanting to see the land of Goethe and Beethoven made great again, even if one doesn't share that view. Shit!"

Fleming had been momentarily distracted by a cyclist riding into the car's path without looking. He slammed on the brakes and hit the horn. Turing was almost as startled as his driver, and it took a few minutes for the two of them to calm down enough to resume their conversation. It was Fleming who managed to bring himself to speak first.

"Bloody cyclists. Absolute menaces. As likely to get killed by one of them as by the Hun. Where were we? Oh yes... Have you ever heard of Tom Driberg?"

"No, I don't believe I have."

"You don't want to. A nasty little spiv, a Communist and a homosexual. But a charmer. Knows everybody."

Turing coughed, embarrassedly, and Fleming looked at him curiously.

"Anyway," Fleming continued, "you've probably read his stuff, even if you don't know it. Writes for the *Express* under the name William Hickey"

"Oh, really? I always thought that was his real name!"

"No, it's a staff name they give to a variety of writers. But Driberg writes most of his stuff. You read it?"

"I've flicked through it. I'm not really an *Express* reader –

more of a *Manchester Guardian* man – but I've always found him quite witty. He's a Communist, you say?"

Fleming nodded. "But he's also a patriot, in his own way. He's not one of those who lets a loyalty to Stalin override his loyalty to the King, which is the important thing."

"Hmm...and you're sure he can be trusted with a job like this?"

"Absolutely. The man is many things, but he's not a traitor. He'll do the job, and keep his own counsel about it. I'd not trust him not to steal sixpence from a blind beggar, but on a job like this he'll manage to be discreet, all right."

They drove on in silence, with both men thinking their own thoughts. Fleming had almost forgotten the reason they'd travelled down in the first place, when Turing spoke up again once more.

"But Ian, what if he's too discreet to actually find the traitors?"

Fleming laughed. "Believe me, that won't be a problem."

Chapter 15

Fleet Street in London is the traditional home of Britain's newspaper industry, and as such it was the place to go if one wanted to meet up with a journalist. More specifically, one would visit one of a number of pubs in the surrounding area, as writing news articles and opinion columns to a tight deadline is often thirsty work.

Ian Fleming sat in one of those pubs, and started to wonder if he should just relocate to London, as he had been spending more time there in the past few weeks than he had in the area in which he was nominally based. This time he was down in the city to see Tom Driberg and to give him the documents from Hess, so that he could "accidentally" let them be found by the right kind of person.

Driberg was a committed anti-Nazi, but he had connections among the right-wing set, and was well known as being able to set aside his own politics if an opportunity for fun came along. What was less well known, outside MI5 circles, was that Driberg was also an agent who had spent much of the previous few years infiltrating the Communist party.

Now that role was more or less over, as he had been unceremoniously dropped by most of the Communist contacts he had so carefully cultivated, and he was sitting in the Bunch of Grapes, just off Fleet Street, nursing a pint of bitter.

Fleming looked at him with something approaching contempt. The man was a high society gadabout, and seeing him slumming it, drinking bitter in an attempt to appear working class, almost made Fleming shudder. Why pretend to be *worse* than you were?

After exchanging perfunctory greetings, the two men had made their way to the snug, where they were unlikely to be disturbed. Fleming disliked doing secret business in public – walls had ears, and careless talk cost lives, as the posters one couldn't avoid seeing hammered home – but the risk was less great than if Driberg had been seen going into a building owned by the security services, and at ten o'clock in the morning the bar was deserted, as even the thirstiest of hacks usually waited at least until lunchtime.

Fleming himself thought that the earlier one had one's first drink of the day, the quicker the hangover from the night before would wear off, and Driberg currently seemed to be of the same opinion. Certainly he appeared already slightly the worse for wear before Fleming had even arrived, although with Driberg appearances could often be deceptive.

Fleming had explained the job to Driberg, but Driberg remained unconvinced,

"So you're asking me to worm my way in with the Fascists now the Communists have kicked me out? You must think I'm far better at espionage than I really am."

"No, I think you already have an in with these people, and that they know you're the kind of person who'd sell out your country for a shilling if you thought it might be amusing."

"Oh charming."

"Come on, Tom. You know your reputation as well as I do. You're a communist, a queer, and a cad. Now, the first two I can forgive, and the last I rather like, but no-one's going to think you're a flag-waving patriot, are they?"

"So what do you want me to do with these papers?"

"Oh, just make sure they get to the right people. You know the types – anyone a little less than keen on our kosher friends. There must be plenty of them among those mumbo-jumbo chanters you hang around with."

Driberg picked up the papers and looked through them, at the endless rows of gibberish.

"So I take it this is in some kind of code?"

Fleming nodded. "Best you not know anything more than that. The less you know, the less damage you can do."

Driberg took a long drag of his cigarette, and blew the smoke towards Fleming's face. Fleming tried not to look aghast at the fact that the man was apparently smoking *Woodbines* now.

"You really expect them to fall for these?" Driberg asked. "For them not to wonder where I got them? They'll know they're forgeries in an instant, and know that I'm trying to trap them."

Fleming sipped his glass of cheap whisky while deciding how to reply, and wondered again what on Earth Driberg thought he was doing pretending to be working class in a place like this. The contrast between Wheatley's club and this bar couldn't have been greater, even though Driberg was of a far better family than Wheatley. Probably one of Driberg's enthusiasms that he'd be over in five minutes, like all the others. Next week, no doubt, Driberg would be pretending to be the illegitimate heir to the throne or something.

He came to the conclusion that it was probably best just to tell Driberg the truth.

"No, they won't know these are forgeries, because they aren't. They're copies, but all the text is taken from the actual papers we captured from Hess."

Driberg boggled. "Why on Earth would you want to hand those to fifth columnists?"

"Because we want to see what they do with them when they have them. There's nothing in there, as far as we can tell, that will actually damage the country, but if we know who gets the papers, and can see what they do with them, we might be able to mop up the whole fifth column in one go."

Driberg looked thoughtfully at Fleming.

"The whole fifth column?"

"Or near as dammit."

"You really think we can do that, with just these papers?"

"I do. This is something we've been setting up for months. Hess walked right into the trap, and now he's given us exactly what we need."

Driberg leaned back in his chair, and took a long drag of his cigarette. He held the smoke in his lungs a while, and then slowly let it out through his nostrils. Then he smiled.

"This could be a hell of a lot of fun, couldn't it, Ian?"

Fleming smiled back. "Oh yes. Definitely your sort of caper."

Driberg took the papers, and said he knew what to do with them.

Chapter 16

A week later, Fleming was beginning to think that he'd made a major mistake in giving the papers to Driberg. No-one — literally nobody — had heard from Driberg since that moment.

He was no longer answering his phone, his door had gone unanswered when Fleming had visited his home, and telegrams and letters had gone unanswered. His column in the *Express* had turned up as normal, but it had read like the kind of column a writer puts in a desk drawer in case it's needed in the future, and a call to the editor had confirmed that Driberg had not spoken to him, either. The column had turned up in the post, with no return address.

In short, it appeared as if Driberg had vanished off the face of the earth. This was not entirely unusual for Driberg — he was not the most reliable of men at the best of times, and was likely to act on a whim without thought for the troubles to which it would put others — but still the coincidence of the timings nagged at Fleming. Perhaps something had happened to Driberg?

But there was no time to worry about Driberg's health and wellbeing — not that the subject would have overly concerned Fleming anyway — as he had arranged to meet up with Wheatley at his club once again, to discuss ideas for dealing with the Hess problem.

Wheatley's reaction to being told of Driberg's disappearance was to give a look so withering that Fleming could almost feel himself cringing.

"You really risked state secrets with that buffoon Driberg?"

"I didn't have a great deal of choice. Anyone in those circles would know that you or I were too sensible. We needed someone a little unpredictable."

"Still. Couldn't you have thought of anyone less likely to disappear on you?"

"Anyone less likely to go AWOL would also have been a less convincing infiltrator. My options were rather limited, you know."

Wheatley nodded. Fleming had a point.

"You do realise that this is almost certainly the work of Aleister Crowley, don't you? We may never see Driberg alive again. He's gone over to the other side."

"The other side? Crowley's on our side, isn't he?"

"On the contrary, Crowley's never on any side but his own. He'll take any opportunity to cause mischief. He and Driberg are alike in that respect, at least. Probably more, if the rumours about Driberg being a queer are true."

"So what do you think Crowley wants with him?"

"Well, it depends very much on what particular hideous practices he's up to at present. I'd be very surprised, though, if this wasn't Crowley's plan from the start. Driberg's a Bolshevik, isn't he?"

"Well, not exactly..."

"Oh come now, don't play games with me. We're not pissing about with definitions here. He's a bolshie."

"He is, but he's also a patriot."

"No such thing as a patriotic socialist. Their only loyalty is to their cause – and right now their great Man of Steel says that the cause is on the side of Adolf."

"Be that as it may, Crowley's no socialist."

"No. He's after power for himself, and he'll be working with the reds and the Germans to get it in whatever way he can."

Wheatley paused to sip his brandy and continued.

"You do realise, don't you, that the Nazis and the Communists are both just faces of a single conspiracy – one that has been meddling in man's affairs for centuries?"

"In man's affairs? What do you mean?"

"I mean that they are both tools of a higher – or should I say lower – power. The beast known to the Carthaginians as Moloch, to the Jews as Baal, and to Christians as the Devil."

"You're joking?"

"I would never joke about such matters. You should know that by now. There are powers in this world which are far beyond men's imaginings, and which work through the shape of history. We are at a great tipping point in history at the moment, my friend, and the scales are tipping towards the dark."

Wheatley took another sip, and continued talking. "Crowley, you see, is a most dangerous fellow. He has experience in espionage, and connections with the leadership of both the Nazis and the Bolshies. He's almost certainly got Driberg involved in his filthy ceremonies. Driberg's not on our side any more. We need someone else to infiltrate Crowley's coven. I'd suggest your young friend Alan."

"Why Turing?"

"Firstly, because he's a young, naive, head-in-the-clouds type. Exactly the kind of man that was always hanging on Crowley's every word. Secondly, because we have to keep this known to as small a group as possible."

Fleming mused on this for a short while, then nodded.

"That makes sense. He does seem the sort that would appeal to Crowley. Someone who he could look clever in front of, but also someone intelligent enough to appreciate that cleverness."

"And he's queer, isn't he?"

"Is he?"

"Oh yes, you can tell a mile off. Disgusting perversion. But Crowley is attracted to that sort."

"Really? He seems quite manly to me. Wouldn't have

thought him the type."

"If there is some disgusting, depraved, practice you can conceive of, Crowley will have engaged in it – along with many you find inconceivable."

"Hmm. Well, you know him better than I do. But I would have said that when I met him he wasn't capable of anything much more strenuous than drinking a weak glass of lemon squash. But I can see that maybe in his younger days he got up to that sort of thing."

Wheatley smiled. "One doesn't lose one's appetites the second one turns forty, you know. And that goes just as well for his type as anyone else. From what I've heard he is still quite active, in his own disgusting way."

"You talk almost as if you admire him for it!"

Wheatley looked disgusted. "Oh Christ no. This isn't about what I like. It's just a fact."

Fleming nodded. He was still not at all happy with this, but he could see the logic of the older man's position.

"So that's it then. We have to send Alan into the den of the Beast." He took another sip of his drink. "I just hope God – and the PM – will forgive us if we lose him."

Chapter 17

Having made the decision to enlist Alan Turing as an undercover operative, Fleming now had to persuade Turing of the wisdom of his plan. On visiting Turing in his office at Bletchley, he found the mathematician less keen on the idea than he had expected.

"So, explain this to me again, Ian, because I really don't think this makes any sense at all."

"You're going undercover."

"I thought Driberg was our undercover operative?"

"He's undercover with the fifth columnists. You'll be under-cover with Crowley."

"But didn't Crowley volunteer to work for our side?"

"He did. But we think he may be a double agent. We need someone on the inside to find out what's going on."

"That's what makes no sense. I'm not a spy. I'm a math-ematician. Getting me to do undercover work would be like getting one of our spies to follow my discussion of the entschei-dungsproblem."

"The what?"

"You take my point."

Fleming nodded. "I do, but that's exactly why I want you to do this. Look, Alan, if my brother Peter turned up asking Crowley about his so-called magic, Crowley would have him down as a spy in an instant. But you? You're an intellectual. You're a bookish sort, and just the kind of person who'd want to get to know Crowley's system."

Turing looked annoyed. "I may be an 'intellectual', but I'm also an empiricist. I value the truth, not this mumbo-jumbo nonsense".

"Yes, I understand that. But Crowley won't know who you are, will he? He'll just see an earnest young man, very quietly spoken and polite, who clearly reads a lot of books and has a sharp mind."

Turing thought. "And you're telling me that there's really no-one in the service who'd be suitable for this? Not a single other person? I find that very hard to believe."

"Well, truth be told, there are people I *could* turn to who could put on a performance that would convince me. But could they convince *Crowley*? He's a wily old bugger, and he clearly understands people far better than I do. I don't want to risk him seeing through someone's disguise. No, the only thing to do is have someone telling as much of the truth about themselves as possible. That means you."

"I'm still not at all convinced this is a wise idea."

"Nor am I. But I honestly don't see any other alternatives. We need someone to infiltrate Crowley's organisation and try to discover what's happened to Tom Driberg."

"Wait a second. . . something's happened to Driberg?"

"We don't know. That's why we need you to investigate. Look, Alan, I'll be as straight with you as I can. Driberg's disappeared. We don't know whether he's been kidnapped, or whether he's just buggered off on holiday for a fortnight without telling anyone, but odds-on it's something to do with the mission. And we think Crowley may have something to do with it."

Turing scratched at the stubble on his chin. "So you want me to go and get involved with someone you think is a kidnapper? I must say, this doesn't sound like the most foolproof of plans."

"It's not. It's a last resort. But if we just send PC Plod

in to arrest Crowley without any evidence, we're likely to never find Driberg alive. The man knows how to keep secrets."

Turing stood up from his chair and started pacing the room restlessly, like a caged animal.

"So you want me to go into a situation that has already claimed at least one agent, despite my utter lack of training. Are you actually mad?"

Fleming sighed. "All right, I'll be completely honest. We think Driberg's gone over to the Bosch's side."

Turing paused in his pacing, and turned to look at Fleming, his mouth open. "He's gone over to the Nazis?"

"We don't know that for sure. But we think it's likely."

"But. . ."

"I know. I would never have thought it of him. But no other explanation makes sense."

"Makes sense of what?"

"Makes sense of his disappearance, makes sense of Crowley, makes sense of anything. It's obvious that Crowley is in league with the Nazis – he was a double agent in the last war, and I'm starting to wonder now if he wasn't actually a triple agent."

"And how do we know it was Crowley who kidnapped him?"

"Well, that's what Dennis thinks."

Turing frowned. "Dennis Wheatley? Hardly the most reliable of people, I'd have said."

"Yes, well, you don't know him. I do. Dennis may rub people up the wrong way on occasion, but without his wisdom and understanding of the world, I'd have been in serious trouble on many occasions. He's a fine man, Alan."

"Hmm. I'll take your word for it, I suppose. He seems like a bit of a buffoon to me, but you know him better than I."

"I do. I'd trust him utterly and implicitly. Anyway, do you have any better ideas as to who kidnapped Driberg, if it wasn't Crowley?"

"Do we even know he's been kidnapped at all?"

"Look, we're getting bogged down here. We know he's disappeared, we think he's been kidnapped, we think that if he was kidnapped it will have been by Crowley. Can we take that as read for the moment and move on?"

"If you wish. I just don't want us going on a wild goose chase."

Fleming sighed.

"Anyway, this is the plan – you go to one of Crowley's lectures, and find a way to have a conversation with him. Pump him for information as best you can without revealing that's what you're doing, and try to get yourself into his organisation. With luck, that should be easy enough for you to manage."

Turing nodded.

"And if I do get lucky enough to join his coven, what should I do then?"

"Use your initiative. Try not to get yourself killed. And report back anything you find. And save Driberg, if that's still possible."

The two men shook hands, and Fleming left Turing to his work.

Chapter 18

The opportunity to meet Crowley turned up only a day or two later. Crowley was making a rare visit to London, to attend a speaking engagement. He had been booked to speak at what appeared to Turing to be a gathering of cranks. The small room in the back of a pub was half-empty, and Turing had no difficulty finding a seat.

While waiting for Crowley, who according to the placard outside the venue was apparently lecturing under the absurd name of "Frater Perdurabo", to arrive, Turing kept himself from boredom by scanning the faces of what passed for a crowd. The group gathered there to hear Crowley talk was exclusively male, and tended towards the extremes of appearance – men with too much or too little hair, either beanpole-thin or practically spherical, and almost all wearing spectacles. Many of them were carrying notebooks, in which they were making notes even before Crowley turned up. Turing tried unobtrusively to look at the notes of the person nearest to him, but quickly decided that the combination of an illegible scrawl and a surfeit of acronyms made it impossible to glean any useful information that way.

Crowley himself, when he arrived, had an odd effect on the crowd. The man himself walked with something of a stoop, and his skin hung off his frame in folds, as if it belonged to a much fatter and much younger man. There was even something of a pungent smell to him, as if he had not bathed as recently as one would expect before a public appearance. Nonetheless, his audience appeared galvanised, unable to look away from this enfeebled old man.

The lecture, entitled "The Soldier and the Hunchback", was apparently one Crowley – who introduced himself as "Sir Aleister Crowley", though Turing was unaware of him ever having received any honours, and thought it unlikely – gave often enough to recite from memory, and with a rather bored expression. Turing was nonetheless mildly impressed. Crowley was clearly intelligent, and at least some of what he said was rather good sense.

Crowley spent the lecture talking about how every question – which he signified with the "hunchback" question mark – must lead to an answer (the straight-backed "soldier" exclamation mark), but that every answer must itself lead to another question, and so on. He was talking about how the point isn't to find a final answer to one's questions, but to enjoy the process of seeking the truth without lust for results.

It seemed remarkably good sense to Turing, especially coming from someone who was supposed to be interested in Yoga and Kabbalah and all the other rot that infected perfectly good minds and ate away at their critical faculties, turning them into mush. Crowley may well have been odd, but at least he understood how to think, and that was a rare commodity.

Certainly, what he was saying struck a chord with Turing. Some of his most important work, after all, had been to prove that there were some questions which were, of their very nature, unanswerable. Not in a mystic way – these weren't profound mysteries to be wondered at – but just questions which had no answers. But progress could still be made, even with no final end in sight.

And progress was what Turing intended to make today. He waited until the end of the talk, and sat through the usual progression of non-questions from the audience with which he was all too familiar as an academic without speaking. It was only as Crowley was leaving the building that Turing approached him.

"Sir Aleister?"

"Do what thou wilt shall be the whole of the law. Can I help you?"

"I just want to say how very inspiring your talk was. 'The method of science, the aim of religion'. That's so much more clear-headed than most of the piffle one hears on this subject."

"Thank you. You will find as you investigate the subject of magick that there are only two categories of people who engage in occult practices. There are those who know much, but do not speak of it; and there are those who know nothing, and make sure that everyone around them knows the fact."

"And which are you?"

Crowley laughed at Turing's audacity. "I? I am above categories, in this and every other area of life."

"So you are in the category of things which are not in a category? You're quite a paradoxical man, then, Mr. Crowley."

Crowley suddenly looked at Turing thoughtfully. "I would say that membership of a category of which one is not a member is only paradoxical if one abides by the hidebound rules of Aristotelianism. I am capable of being neither one thing nor the other, and both at once, and will not be tied down by mere syllogisms. I wonder, are you similarly flexible, Mr...?"

"Turing. Alan Turing. I'm a mathematician."

"I am very pleased to meet you, Mr Turing. It's refreshing to find someone of your training with a mind open enough to appreciate the lessons of magick. How have you come to take an interest in the occult arts?"

"Well, I'm only just starting to learn about this stuff, but I'm interested in the Kabbalah. Am I right in thinking it's all about seeing the hidden patterns behind the world? Using permutations and combinations of numbers and letters to unlock the code that is the apparent world and see the underlying reality?"

"To an extent, yes. Although what one tends to find is not a final reality, but merely another imitation. Every answer just brings another question."

"Isn't that always the case?"

"Oh, you'd be very surprised, Mr. Turing...or perhaps, actually, you wouldn't be as surprised as you might appear. You strike me as someone who has more hidden layers than most."

Turing raised an eyebrow. "Me? Oh, I don't know about that. I'm pretty much an open book."

"That may well be the case. But even an open book can be impossible to read, if one does not understand the language in which it is written...or if it is written in a cipher to which one does not possess the key."

"I assure you, Sir Aleister, that my secrets require no key to unlock."

Crowley chuckled. "We shall see. We shall see." He reached into his jacket pocket and took out a business card. "If you would do me the kindness of visiting me at home tomorrow, we can discuss this further. But for now, Mr. Turing, I must bid you goodnight."

Crowley left, and Turing looked at the card. The text was written entirely in symbols.

Chapter 19

A prison cell after lights-out is always dark, and during a black-out, when the entire city was dark, and on a night when storm clouds were gathering, this particular cell was a place of almost Stygian blackness.

Rudolf Hess was alone in his cell, and no observer could have seen him anyway, though he still kept his hands above the bed covers, having already become acculturated to prison life and the guards' demands to see what he was doing at all times. But had there been an observer with the second sight watching over him, that observer may have noticed his fingers twitch, making the shape of a pentagram atop the covers.

Hess knew now that the Führer had disowned him, called him a madman. That was to be expected. It had to appear as if his mission had been a failure. But Hess remembered the look in the Führer's eyes the last time they'd spoken. He had only told the Führer of his plans telepathically, of course, but he knew the truth.

The Führer approved, he knew it. No other possibility could even be considered. Hess' actions were the Führer's will, in prison just as much as they had been when he had been in the Reichstag, or the beer cellar. He existed only to do what the Führer wanted. And that meant that anything he did *must* be the Führer's will, by definition.

They would be together again, and he would be at the Führer's side, once the plan had been completed. He was going to be a hero of the Reich.

He lay there in the cold, dark, room, so much less than what he had become used to when he was the Führer's most trusted associate. While the room was better than his previous cell, it still stunk of England. Every country had its own smell, in Hess' experience, and England's was one of mould, damp, and decay. The cold and the stink did not bother him, though. He had been in prison before, and he knew he could stand it. Of course, back then, he'd had the Führer with him, and that had been some consolation. . .

But that had been before he had learned of the true, secret, reality, the horror that was behind the visible world. He knew the Führer had always understood that, though as with much else they shared they had never spoken of it. It had taken Hess longer to grasp the realities that had driven the Führer on, but once he had seen the truth, he could not unsee it.

He muttered to himself, a few phrases in an ancient tongue. His lips stumbled over the words at first, as if the unfamiliar syllables with their guttural consonants did not want to leave his mouth.

The Führer had planned this all along, he was sure of it. The Führer had never wanted to go to war with the British Empire – what true German could possibly wish war with a people so similar to the Germanic? And only a madman would want to confront the most powerful empire the world had ever seen. No, the Führer was a man who wanted only friendship with the British. And Hess' task had been to secure that friendship.

His hands twitched again. Was that a spark from his left forefinger?

He had been entrusted with the most sacred task imaginable. The fate of the whole Aryan race, and of the Reich, had rested upon him. He had accomplished the major part of his Great Work, and now there was only one task left ahead, before he could enjoy his well-earned rest. After this, let the British do their worst. His reward was a higher one than mere earthly punishments could destroy.

Fleming. . . yes, he would definitely pay, no matter what happened. The Englishman had implied that he would. . . no, no, he wouldn't even allow himself to think of the disgusting, degrading, filth that the Englishman had dared to suggest between him and his beloved Führer. The Englishman would be forced to pay for that insinuation.

The muttering had become a chant. Still under his breath, still quiet, but now the words had their own rhythm, almost a music, which carried him along almost despite himself now.

When the time came, he was ready to die for the Aryan race; to subsume his will in a greater one, and to become one with a greater power. That time was not yet, however, and for now he had his part to play in ensuring the triumph of the German people.

But when that time did come, he knew it would not be the end for him. Not for him the non-existence of the lesser races. He had a far grander fate in store. By giving his will over to the highest possible power, by eliminating his own desires and living only to serve, he could eventually become one with the infinite.

He continued whispering, feeling a static charge build up in the air around him. The hairs on his arms started to stand on end, and he could hear a strange echo of his words as he spoke them, as if the magickal ritual were being spoken by a second voice, a fraction after his own.

His head tipped back, his eyes rolled back in his head, and he continued to recite. His voice grew louder and louder, he started to gesture with his fingers, and a strange glow emanated from him. He almost looked as if he was moving out of himself – a strange doubling of his appearance. His muttering raised in volume, slowly becoming audible speech, which in turn grew in volume until he was shouting, howling.

The guards came running into the cell, to find him screaming strange syllables, unlike anything in either the German or

English language, into the air. His face seemed blurred, whether because of the mist that had entered the room or for some other reason they couldn't tell. They moved to restrain him, but as they got to him he went silent. His head dropped forward, and his eyes appeared blank. Whatever force had been animating him had gone.

Rudolph Hess was still there, but his mind was somewhere far away.

Chapter 20

Turing's trip to Torquay was rather more eventful than Fleming's had been. As someone who was used to travelling by bicycle rather than by car, he had made his way down by train. Given the many problems the train companies were having in getting a reliable service, this had meant that a journey of a couple of hundred miles had taken the best part of a day, and he found himself arriving at Crowley's doorstep as the midsummer sun was finally setting.

He had cycled from the train station, and was now bitterly regretting the decision. While he was an athletic man by temperament, he was also one who didn't enjoy the heat, and the stifling hot sea air had made him feel like he was choking to death at times — the humid air had felt like he was inhaling steam, and had mingled with the smell of his own sweat from the overheated, stuffy, train carriage he'd been in.

He'd expected before leaving that the bicycle ride would calm his nerves after the stress of the train, and allow him to clear his head and maybe get some real work done. He'd forgotten to take into account the hilliness of that part of the west country, and the consequent strain on his legs.

Oh well, he'd arrived, at least.

He knocked, and the door was answered by Crowley, but this was not the same man he'd seen give the lecture. Oh, it was the same body, no doubt, but while the person he'd seen in London was a gaunt, tired, elderly man, Crowley now had a new animating spirit – he was alive and aware in a way he hadn't been at the earlier meeting.

"Do what thou wilt shall be the whole of the law."

"Love is the law, love under will."

Crowley gestured for Turing to enter, and closed the door behind the two of them.

"Ah, so you've been paying attention to my writings then? Many of your friends refuse to use the correct greetings when addressing me."

"Which friends are those?"

"Mr. Fleming, for example, who visited me a few days ago."

Turing tried unsuccessfully to hide his shock.

"I'm sorry, I think you must have me confused with somebody else. I don't know a Mr. Fleming."

Crowley laughed. "Oh really? You'd have me believe your turning up here is just a coincidence? Very well. Do come through to the sitting room."

The two men walked through to a small, sparsely decorated room. Crowley walked over to a drinks cabinet and took out a decanter. He poured himself a glass of whisky, and gestured with the decanter towards Turing, raising his eyebrows. Turing shook his head, and Crowley put the stopper back in the decanter.

"I see that you are a sceptic."

"I beg your pardon?"

"You are a non-believer."

"I wouldn't say that."

"I would. It is no matter. As I have said many times, our method is science, our aim religion. If magick is not powerful enough to convince the sceptical, then it has no power at all. I shall convince you in time; I am sure of it. In the meantime, let me know what it is you wish to discover. And do, please, take a seat. If you continue standing there with your hands behind your back like that I shall become convinced you are a policeman."

Turing sat, and having become aware of his hands he folded them neatly on his lap. Then he realised what he had just done, unfolded them, and crossed his legs, resting his right hand on his knee. He wished he'd taken Crowley up on the offer of whisky, just to have something to do with his hands, and he suspected that that was precisely the effect Crowley had intended.

"I'm glad to see you were able to follow the directions on my card."

"A fairly simple cipher to break, since I knew that your own name would be encoded."

"Oh no doubt. A mild joke, not a real test. Of course, I have had some time since our discussion to look into your work. Your paper on the halting problem was most remarkable, though of course a trivial extension of Gödel's work."

Turing was surprised. "You know Gödel's paper?"

Crowley nodded. "I try to keep up with the latest developments. Of course, I am an amateur dabbler, but I find an understanding of mathematical logic a necessity for any man who wishes to think clearheadedly."

"I should not have thought that you would approve of my results."

Crowley smiled. "On the contrary, they delight me. Your paper shows that there will always be more unanswered questions, that we shall never fall into the trap of dull certitude. There will always be more hunchbacks than there are soldiers – possibly an infinity of them! How should any man greet that prospect but with delight?"

"Many did not greet it with delight. At least, when Gödel wrote his paper, they were absolutely distraught at the incompleteness of mathematics. My own paper, as you say, is an extension of his."

"Ah, but the implications! The implications are so very different!"

"How so?"

"Gödel's work is in terms of statements, and he merely states that there are some true statements that are unprovable. Any man can see that. I can say I breakfasted on kippers this morning. Can I prove it? No."

"But I suppose it's true."

"Actually, I had an egg. But the point is, Gödel only shows that there are true things we cannot prove. You, on the other hand, show that there are questions we cannot answer."

"The two statements are equivalent, surely?"

"If that were true, you should not have published your paper. And yet you did. All of mathematics, my dear Alan – I may call you Alan, mayn't I?"

Turing nodded.

"All of mathematics is tautological in nature. We have some premises; from those premises we draw conclusions. The only conclusions we can possibly draw are those which are implicit in the premises. Yet we come up with fascinating new ideas."

"I agree, of course. But I still don't think the implications of my work are all that different."

"Oh, but they are. Gödel talks of mathematics. His work is in the Platonic realm of pure thought. You talk of machinery, of practicality. Your machine is the word made flesh. Your work is a bridge between the material and the spiritual."

Turing opened his mouth to reply, but Crowley quickly continued. "Fascinating as this discussion is, the hour draws late, and I am not the nocturnal beast I once was. Shall we continue on the morrow? Come, I shall show you to your room."

Turing, who had been expecting to have to find a boarding-house for the night, nodded mutely and followed the older man upstairs.

Chapter 21

Tom Driberg woke up with a groan, his head hurting badly. What had he been drinking? Surely whatever it was it couldn't have caused a hangover this bad? This was worse than any he'd had in years. His head was aching, and there was an acidic taste in the back of his throat, and a burning sensation that suggested he had vomited in the recent past.

But something was not quite right – there was a lingering, sweet, smell in his nostrils, too, which he wouldn't have expected from a hangover.

Oh well, nothing for it but to open the eyes. He did so cautiously, wincing in anticipation at the expected brightness, but surprisingly enough the room he was in appeared to be darkened.

He rubbed his head, and looked around at the small, bare, room he found himself in, and he remembered.

It wasn't the drink. He'd been knocked out with some sort of noxious gas. He remembered being in a long, seemingly friendly, discussion with one of the people he'd been investigating, when suddenly a hand had reached out from behind him and smothered him. He'd struggled, but had quickly gone under.

He tried to sit up, and found he couldn't. He had no energy or strength left in the muscles in his torso. Whatever it was that had knocked him out, it must have been powerful stuff. He decided the best thing to do would be to pretend to still be unconscious, at least until he knew what was going on.

He wondered what Fleming would say to do in a situation like this. Probably not to get oneself into such a situation in the first place, he supposed. Ian was often a source of good advice, but it was impractical in the extreme.

He continued to play dead, waiting for his captors to reveal themselves. He would escape, of course – he had no doubt of that. He'd been in worse scrapes before, and no doubt would be again. But the most important thing to do when trying to escape was to make a plan. It would be hours, perhaps days, before he was sure enough of his surroundings to make a break for it.

In the meantime, he could try to figure out, as best he could, where he was and who had captured him. Of course, he had a fair idea of the answer to the latter question – the people he was investigating had figured out he was working for British intelligence – but the former question needed some work. Was he going to be able to escape?

There was a conversation happening outside the door. It was muffled, but Driberg could just about make out the words if he kept himself quiet. There were two voices, both of them men, and both educated.

"Is everything in hand?"

"It is. We still need to select the sacrifice, but should no-one suitable volunteer for the honour, we can always use the prisoner."

"I was wondering why we were bothering to keep him alive. Does he really deserve such a supreme gift? We'll make him a martyr."

"It doesn't matter. Let him be a martyr if he chooses. He is, after all, going to die either way. He might as well die happy. Remember, he's British. He's not the real enemy."

"Well, he's hardly a friend, either, is he?"

"That's not the point. We kill British people only if we have to. We're not barbarians. But someone has to die, and if we don't get a willing sacrifice we go for the other type."

"The stones will run with blood, and the Saxon volk will once again be supreme."

This didn't sound good. Driberg wasn't keen on the idea of stones running with blood, and certainly not with his own blood, which he preferred to keep in his own blood vessels where at all possible. And as for martyrdom, that had always been very far down the list of Driberg's ambitions. No, this wasn't good at all.

Something dangerous was going on, and he needed to discover precisely what. But he couldn't do that from within his cell. The question was whether his captors' plan really did involve human sacrifice. He'd thought he was infiltrating fascists, not a witches' coven.

First of all, he had to figure out whether he had been meant to hear that conversation or not. It seemed too coincidental that his captors would have the conversation close enough for him to hear it, unless they wanted to send him a message. But what message could it be?

Were they perhaps trying to get him scared enough of being sacrificed that he would be willing to spill secrets? Surely they knew that wouldn't work. But what else could they do?

He realised that there were only two possible outcomes to his imprisonment that could satisfy his captors. They would either convert him to their cause – or at least believe they had done so – or they would kill him. They couldn't let him go, and they certainly weren't going to keep him locked up indefinitely – he'd have too many chances to escape, and if nothing else they wouldn't want to share their food rations any longer than they had to.

So the conversation had been, as far as it went, accurate then. They were going to kill him. Which meant that it was entirely possible that the stuff about sacrifice had also been true. Quite what purpose it would serve the Nazis to sacrifice him, he didn't know, but he didn't intend to stick around and find out.

He had to figure out what resources he had to work with. He looked around the room – nothing except his own clothes, the door, and the contents of his pockets. He checked through them, and discovered that his wallet, watch, and keys all remained present. His captors may have been thugs, but apparently they weren't thieves.

Of course, that was unsurprising. He'd recognised one of the voices, and it wasn't one he'd have expected to find among the debauched Bohemian lesser aristocracy whose fashionable fascism he'd attempted to infiltrate. What was Lord Keynsham, of all people, doing in this company?

Chapter 22

The dawn light through the window woke Turing earlier than he was accustomed to rising. Although he was at his best in the mornings, he was still used to sleeping in a room with shutters to prevent any light from leaking through, and had not realised quite how thin the curtains in Crowley's spare room had been until floral-patterned shadows fell upon his eyelids at not much past four in the morning.

He groaned and put the pillow over his eyes, determined to wait as long as possible before acknowledging that he had been woken. There was no reason for anyone to be up at this hour, especially not when they were on holiday, or at least as close as Turing was going to get to a holiday while the war was on.

That Crowley had a spare room at all was a rare luxury to Turing's mind, as every bedroom, attic, and even shed for miles around Bletchley was occupied by people who had been moved to work on the interception and decryption of German messages. Turing decided to wait until after breakfast before contacting Fleming.

It was five hours after he awoke that Turing finally made the phone call. In that time five cups of strong coffee had managed to erase the worst of his morning tiredness, and the conversation with Crowley over breakfast had taken care of the rest of it, so when he finally decided to cal Fleming it was in a state of excitement. He was almost hopping up and down in the phone box as he waited for an answer. After four or five rings, the phone was answered.

"Fleming."

"It's Alan. It worked, Ian!"

"What did you discover, if it's safe to talk about on the telephone?"

"I've not discovered anything yet, but I'm to be initiated into the Ordo Templi Orientis by Crowley himself in a couple of days. He's going to tell me everything then – give me access to the order's inner secrets and hidden teachings!".

"Really?"

"Oh yes. He seems quite eager. The order has apparently been getting fewer and fewer new members in recent years, and he said they're always after new blood. I'll be initiated in a few days, apparently."

"And what does initiation involve?"

"Oh, the swearing of fearsome oaths, no doubt. But I'm not scared of whatever hocus-pocus ritual he has us go through."

The line went quiet. After a few seconds, Turing broke the silence.

"Ian, are you still there?"

"Oh, yes. Yes. Sorry, I was miles away. Just wondering if Dennis knows anything about these initiation rites. It may well be that he can warn you of anything you need to prepare for."

"Oh, I shouldn't worry about that. It'll be harmless enough. He's a doddering old man, not a wrestler."

Fleming's tone of voice seemed to suggest a certain dubiousness about this. "Look, Alan, I trust your judgement of course – I wouldn't have sent you down there if I didn't – but are you absolutely sure that this is the wisest course of action?"

"Ian, you sent me down here to do just this! This is why I'm here!"

"Still. I expected you to talk to him for a couple of hours, get into his good books. I didn't expect you to go all the way to joining his coven and dancing naked in the moonlight!"

"Gosh! Is that really the sort of thing they get up to, then?"

"Oh, I don't know. But I imagine so. Anyway, my point is that I didn't expect things to move so quickly."

"But isn't that a good thing?"

"Oh, rather. But one doesn't want to be too hasty."

Turing looked out through the windows of the phone box, and studied the streets. There were a few cyclists and elderly people walking their dogs through the cobblestoned roads, but on the whole this was almost deserted. He couldn't understand why a man such as Crowley would end up in the middle of nowhere like this.

He scratched himself and breathed through his mouth, trying to stop the smell of the phone box from getting in through his nose. Like all phone boxes, it had been used as an impromptu public urinal by local drunkards, and Turing was almost overpowered by the smell. He wondered what other unsavoury activities the box had played host to.

He realised after a few seconds that he had been daydreaming, and that Fleming had been talking.

"Sorry, old man. Drifted off there for a second. What was it you were saying?"

"I was saying that I think we need Dennis' advice on this."

"Why? Surely he can't be of any assistance here."

"He knows more about Crowley than any of the rest of us do."

Turing went on to tell Fleming that in his opinion, Crowley was far more reasonable than Fleming believed — he suspected that Crowley wasn't in league with the Nazis at all, although of course he would keep his eye out.

"Frankly, he seems far too egocentric to want to be part of someone else's personality cult."

"Are you sure?"

"Well, of course one can't be absolutely certain. But he seems more interested in his own 'law of Thelema' than in anything to do with the war. The man lives inside his own head, and doesn't venture out of it to look at the world around him at all any more, if indeed he ever did."

"Hmm. I'm still not entirely convinced, but I'll take your word for it for now."

"So, do you have any more information for me? The more I know, the better I can deal with Crowley."

"Nothing I can tell you over the telephone, and nothing that won't wait until we can talk in person anyway. I plan to see our mutual friend again later, and I shall certainly pass on any information that seems pertinent. Expect a cable from me soon."

Turing fiddled nervously with the cord of the telephone.

"Ian. . . you're sure there's really nothing to Crowley's magic, aren't you?"

"Of course I am! I'd have thought you would be too."

"Oh, I am. I am. It's just. . ."

"Just what?"

"Well, he looked a good ten years younger this morning than he did last night."

Chapter 23

Driberg needed to get out, and fast.

His captors had come to the room a couple of hours earlier, to bring him what passed for food and drink, and to ask him if he required the lavatory, an offer he had eagerly accepted. The problem was that they had done so without covering their faces. They were clearly not worried that he would ever be in a position to give their descriptions to the police.

If that was the case, there were only two possibilities. The first was that they intended to convert him to their cause – something Driberg had to admit was vanishingly unlikely given the circumstances. The other, and the conclusion to which he was reluctantly but compellingly drawn, was that they thought he would never have the opportunity to talk to anyone.

There was no doubt in his mind now – these people really did intend to kill him. He was going to be sacrificed in one of their rituals to their dark gods, for purposes he couldn't begin to comprehend. But his captors' reasoning was of little interest to him anyway. What was of interest was getting out.

The room he was in offered little in the way of opportunity. It was totally bare, just floorboards and a sloping roof, with one door that was locked from the outside. Other than a couple of sheets and a pillow, there was nothing in there that could be used as an escape tool, and there wasn't even a window for him to dangle out of using the sheets as a rope.

If you can't make use of objects, you have to make use of

people. What he needed to do was to get the attention of a guard. The guards would have to be manipulated – or forced – into letting him out of the room. Even if it was only to go to the lavatory, that would still give him more opportunity to get free.

But how to get their attention? Driberg considered, but quickly decided against, the idea of faking illness. Doubtless the guards had seen the same films as he had, and anyway his health didn't seem to be a particular concern to them. The idea of wishing to use the lavatory again was more promising, but there was always the danger of them merely providing him with a chamberpot.

Would they give the condemned man a fag? That might be worth trying, though it still wouldn't get him out of the room. But it might give him some opportunity to have a conversation, at least – sound out the guards and see if anything came up. Worth a try – and if nothing else, at least he might get a fag out of it.

"I say! Anyone got a gasper?"

There was no answer. Driberg started to bang on the door. "You there! Is there anyone there? Service!"

He heard muffled footsteps coming towards the door, and a male voice responded. "What?"

Driberg decided to play up his upper-class mannerisms, in the hope that this would give him an air of authority.

"I say! You chaps wouldn't happen to have a fag you could lend a chap would you? I'm gasping in here."

There was a pause. "A fag?"

"That's right."

"One second." Driberg could hear the sound of keys in a lock, and the door opened a crack. He could make out a male figure in the dim light.

"It's only a Woodbine, will that do?" asked the guard.

"Better than nothing. You got a light as well?"

"Yeah," the guard patted his pockets. As Driberg's eyes

grew accustomed to the light, he was able to make out the guard's face. If he wasn't hiding his face, that was a worrying sign for Driberg's future. The guard finally found his matchbox. "Here you go."

Driberg reached for the matchbox, but instead of taking it he grabbed the guard's hand, yanking his arm round behind his back. The guard yelled, but Driberg quickly clamped a second hand over his mouth. The guard tried to bite, but Driberg held firm. He pushed forward on the guard's back, keeping hold of his hand, and slammed his head against the door frame. The guard went limp in his arms.

Driberg patted the guard down, and found a revolver in an inside jacket pocket. He took it out and said a silent prayer of thanks, then quickly oriented himself. He was on a small balcony with a flight of stairs leading down, so the only reasonable course was to go down the stairs. He took his shoes off and held them in one hand, and crept down in his stockinged feet, trying his damnedest not to make a sound.

There was a guard stood at the bottom of the stairwell, thankfully looking the other way, so Driberg didn't have to shoot him. Instead, when he got to the third stair from the bottom, Driberg held the barrel of the gun and hit the guard on the head, as hard as he could, with the butt of the gun. Driberg almost cried out himself from the gun barrel digging hard into his hand as he hit the guard, but the guard didn't make a sound, just crumpled to the ground.

Was that it? Could it be that simple to escape? Apparently so. Driberg wondered if the lack of guards was a lack of planning on his captors' behalf, or was it something else? Could they be hoping for him to escape – perhaps what he'd overheard was misinformation, designed to lead the Government down a false trail? Or, indeed, were they so certain of their plan's success at this point that there was no need to keep him under heavy guard? Maybe he no longer presented any danger.

Whatever the reason, he was grateful. He didn't have the

temperament for captivity.

Driberg looked around, but no-one else came running, and the way was clear. He ran to the front door, drew back the bolts, and threw the door open. Outside it was pouring down with rain, but he welcomed even that as a blessing compared to being locked inside. He ran out into the rain, ecstatic and free.

Chapter 24

Fleming spent much of the rest of the day content with how things were progressing, and it wasn't until he visited Wheatley at his home that evening, to have a quiet drink and discuss how the operation was proceeding, that he became disquieted.

Fleming gave Wheatley a brief précis of the conversation he'd had with Turing earlier that day, and was horrified when, as he got to the point of the story in which Turing was joining the OTO, Wheatley interrupted.

"You damned fool! You damned, incompetent, blithering, fool!"

"What the hell are you talking about?"

"Can't you see? He's going to be Crowley's midsummer sacrifice! Your young friend Alan will be dead unless we stop them."

Fleming was horrified.

"You mean to tell me that Crowley will sacrifice *human beings*? What kind of monster is he?"

"Oh, he talks about it quite openly."

Wheatley got up from his chair and walked over to a bookcase, on which Fleming could see a curious mixture of leatherbound copies of serious works of literature, a handful of Penguins, and rather a lot of the more lurid sort of thriller, all jumbled together in an order that only Wheatley could possibly have understood, if indeed even he did. Wheatley looked at the books for a moment, pulled out a copy of a book entitled

Magick, and pointed Fleming to a marked passage. Fleming read, horrified.

"'For the highest spiritual working one must accordingly choose that victim which contains the greatest and purest force. A male child of perfect innocence and high intelligence is the most satisfactory and suitable victim.' The man's a maniac! What are we to do?"

"What we have to do, my dear friend, is to rescue young Alan. We only have two nights in which to do so."

"Two nights? Why two nights?"

"Because two nights from now is the summer solstice. It is absolutely certain that Crowley will kill Turing at dawn on that night."

"Is it really only two nights until the solstice? Time's flying. It seems like only yesterday that Hess landed, and yet that was in early May."

"It was well over a month ago now. They've had more than enough time to prepare everything except their sacrifice – and then you went and handed them one on a plate. I still can't believe you could be quite so stupid."

"But, hang on, this says a male *child*. Alan's not a child – he's not much younger than me."

"Oh, that's a trifling matter. Crowley would kill a child for preference, of course, but the important thing as I understand it is the intelligence – and in that your young friend Turing certainly qualifies admirably. And it would be just like Crowley to make the sacrifice serve another purpose, and get rid of a troublemaker."

Fleming took a sip of whisky and let the smokey taste fade away in his mouth while he contemplated the situation they found themselves in. To lose one undercover operative was bad enough – to lose a second, one who had knowledge vital to the war effort, would be utterly unthinkable.

At this rate the Germans were going to be able to take over the whole country without even having to invade, simply by kidnapping British agents or winning them over to their revolting cultish practices.

"We need to do something. Where will this ceremony be held?"

"Crowley won't want to travel far. He's already been up to town once this month, and it's possible that he made arrangements for the sacrifice while he was here, but London's simply too busy for the ritual to go unnoticed. Far more likely, I think, that he'll be in Torquay or thereabouts. We must head there immediately."

"You're that certain he's going to be killed?"

"I'd stake my own life on it. You read the ritual. They need a willing volunteer, but they're not going to waste any of their own people on it. A new recruit like Alan would be absolutely perfect for them."

"Is there any chance we can save him?"

"It's still possible, if we're lucky. They won't do anything to him before the sacrifice – the pure sacrifice must be completely intact in body. Just pray God we are not too late to stop this monstrosity."

"How can men do such monstrous things?"

"You ask that in the middle of a war like this? Men are animals, Ian. Some of us have a thin veneer of civilisation, but underneath we are little more than baboons, more than willing to tear apart any member of the pack who doesn't fit in."

"I know. And God knows I've done my own share of things I'm not proud of to serve the King. But that's just it – I did it to serve my country. What on Earth can possess people like Crowley?"

"Oh, nothing on Earth possesses him. It's the very Devil himself. The Devil offers worldly power, and traps men into committing acts that destroy their souls. Once their souls are gone, Satan – or Moloch, or Baal, call him what you will – enters their body."

"You mean that literally, don't you? You really think that the

Devil himself has a presence in this world, that he is personally causing all this."

"After all we have seen so far, how can you doubt it?"

"It could just be that men let their worse natures take over."

"And what else do we mean by our worse natures than the Devil?"

"I take your point."

Wheatley got up and pondered his bookcase again for a moment, as if he was trying to find a particular book. Eventually, he must have found what he was looking for, as he pulled a large, leather-bound, volume from the shelf and handed it to Fleming.

Fleming looked at it curiously.

"What is this? *The Book of the Law*? What's that?"

Wheatley smiled. "That book, my young friend, is to Crowley's movement what *Mein Kampf* is to Hitlerism and *Das Kapital* to the reds. Read that, and you will understand Crowley's mind. And then you will wish you hadn't."

Fleming opened the book, and started to read.

Chapter 25

The book was only short, and Fleming had read it in a matter of an hour. He put it down white-faced with horror.

"This. . . this is a manifesto for utter anarchy. For destruction of the whole world. The man thinks himself a God!"

"Yes, yes he does," Wheatley replied, "and remember these are only his outer teachings. Whatever he teaches his inner circle, it is surely worse."

Now that time was of the essence, Fleming and Wheatley needed to get as much information as they could. They arranged to rendezvous in three hours, and Fleming went off determined to find out from Hess what was going on, beating it out of him if necessary.

On the drive to the Tower, Fleming fumed to himself. All of this — two good men disappeared, one gone over to the darkness, one to be sacrificed to Satan — had been caused by the man he was going to see. Never mind Hess' complicity in the Nazis' crimes, Fleming was furious at what he'd done to his friends.

He knew that anger wouldn't be helpful — what he needed was to get information from Hess, about what was going on, and what Crowley's role in it all was, and he knew that being angry would only make that more difficult. At the same time, he suspected that any emotional state at all would be useless in obtaining information.

He went over his plan for the interview in his head, trying

to get clear exactly what it was that he needed to discover from Hess. He needed the names of his British accomplices, obviously – not the ones who had been British agents, but the ones who were now kidnapping people – but he also needed to find out what the point of all this was.

By the time he got to the Tower, he knew exactly what he had to say, and what he had to do to get a response from Hess. Or so he thought.

When he entered Hess' cell, the German was sitting upright, facing towards the cell wall. He did not turn when Fleming came in, or even acknowledge him in any way.

"Prisoner Hess?"

There was no answer.

"Prisoner Hess, on your feet when a British officer enters the room!"

There was still no movement, and Hess continued to face the wall, unmoving.

"Guards!"

Two guards rushed in. "What's the matter, sir?" asked one.

"The prisoner. He's refusing to move."

The guards walked over to Hess, grabbed him by both shoulders, and turned him to face Fleming. Hess' face was blank, and utterly expressionless. It looked like all the muscles had had their nerve connections cut – his jaw was open, his cheeks were sagging, and he wasn't even blinking.

Fleming waved his hand in front of the prisoner's face, looking for any response at all, but Hess' eyes remained firmly fixed straight ahead. Attempting to get any response at all, he took a punch at the Nazi's crotch, but Hess didn't even flinch.

"The man's catatonic. We need to get a doctor out to him straight away. Probably drugged himself."

The idea of getting medical help for Hess revolted Fleming's every instinct – the man was a Nazi and a coward, and as far as Fleming was concerned he deserved to rot, but he couldn't be allowed to die until he'd given Britain all the information he held about the Germans' war plans. So for now, at least, he required medical attention.

The doctor came and examined Hess as best he could, given the subject's utter lack of co-operation. The examination revealed that Hess was still breathing and his heart was still beating, but there were no other signs of life – no reflex action, no blink response. It was as if Hess was dead, but somehow still breathing.

Fleming had never seen anything like this. He'd thought at first that it might be some sort of trick, but no-one could be so good an actor that he could withstand this kind of examination.

"How can this happen?" Fleming asked the doctor. "Has he poisoned himself? Has he had some kind of a stroke? What can cause this?"

"I can't know for sure. There are several possible explanations – he could have mesmerised himself, put himself in some sort of a trance, for example. But my guess is that it's something more serious – he may have had a stroke, or sustained some kind of organic brain damage. There's no way of telling – all we can do is hope he pulls out of it."

Fleming wanted to scream. He knew how to get information out of a prisoner – there wasn't a man in the world who could completely resist giving away *some* secrets, and Fleming knew better than most how to get crucial details to slip – but there was no way to do the impossible, and a man who is incapable of talking will not reveal anything.

In any other circumstances, this wouldn't matter so much. There's no such thing as a total secret, and anything one man knows another surely does. With any other prisoner, Fleming would have moved on to other sources of the same information. There's always another way to discover the truth, if you need it badly enough.

As it was, he had found himself actually hoping for the recovery of a Nazi – for a medical miracle to allow the return to health of Hitler's second-in-command! What strange mental worlds the exigencies of war led one into.

But he now knew there was no hope, at least in the time he had available. Hess was not going to talk and he had no other source for the information he needed.

So Fleming was stuck. He was up against a time limit and his one lead was catatonic. There was no choice left to him. He'd have to meet up with Wheatley, get down to the south-west coast, and confront Crowley, all within a few hours. This was now a race against time, and one Fleming wasn't at all sure he could win.

Chapter 25

Driberg had managed to get himself back to London. He'd had to hitch-hike, but it turned out that the house in which he had been held captive was only a dozen or so miles from a friend's country home, and he'd been able to cadge a lift and a few cigarettes without too much difficulty.

Stopping only to shave, wash, and put on a clean suit, he made his way to Whitehall, and to the office of Maxwell Knight, to let him know what had transpired during his captivity.

He entered the room without waiting for Knight's secretary to give him permission. Knight was on the telephone, but hung up as soon as he saw Driberg come in. He stood up to take Driberg's hand.

"Tom! How the devil are you? Where have you been?"

"Oh, you know, the usual. Captured by the baddies, fearless escape, home in time for tea. You know how it goes."

Knight laughed. "Be serious, Tom."

"Oh, I'm completely serious at all times, old boy."

"Beg pardon?"

Driberg sat down – he hadn't yet been offered a seat, but he considered that after his recent ordeal he was entitled to sit if he damn well pleased – and took his cigarette case out of his jacket pocket. He pulled one out and lit it, and offered the case to Knight, who shook his head impatiently.

Driberg slowly and carefully put the case back in his pocket. He leaned back and took a drag of his cigarette, making Knight wait for his revelation.

"I was kidnapped, and held prisoner. By Lord Keynsham."

"Keynsham? But he's a buffoon. I wouldn't have thought he had it in him to kidnap anyone"

"He's a buffoon who has managed to persuade most of the Nazis that he's on their side. He's a very dangerous man, Max."

"So what did you learn before you escaped?"

He quickly let Knight know what had been going on. "I was held in an abandoned cottage, somewhere in Kent – I could give you the details, but I imagine it's been cleared out by now."

"I think I need a drink. You care to join me?"

"I wouldn't say no."

Knight got up and walked to the small drinks cabinet in his office, and poured two large glasses of brandy. He handed one to Driberg, who took a small sip and let it linger on his tongue before telling Knight the rest of the story.

He was surprised to see that Knight remained calm when informed of the planned magickal ritual, and only finally expressed any surprise when told of the intended result.

"You're joking?"

"I've never been more serious in my life. They're planning to destroy the whole British Empire, using some mixture of hocus-pocus and voodoo. No idea if it'll work or not, because I have no way of knowing the power of the people involved."

"I read the ritual. Turing translated the papers before we handed them off to you. It'll work all right."

Driberg was not one to show his emotions when confronted with something completely unexpected, and so he only raised one eyebrow quizzically.

"You think they could do some real damage with their magic?"

"Oh, I have no doubt at all on that score. That ritual was created by someone with as much occult knowledge as any man I've ever met. Certainly more than you and I have."

"More than Sir Aleister?"

"At least as much as him. It's not Crowley's work, of course – I know his style well enough to know that – but it has something of the same intelligence to it. The smallest possible sacrifice to get the largest possible effect. It's quite devastatingly cunning stuff."

"No, that doesn't sound like Crowley. He's far more concerned with putting on a show than with getting any effect. Most of his work is absolute rot."

"Oh, believe me, that 'rot' does work. I've seen it with my own eyes, on many occasions. It doesn't always immediately cause manifestations on the physical plane, but if you know what you're looking for you'll always see some evidence, and very soon you'll see exactly what the magician intended."

"Wait. . . you're seriously telling me that he might be able to do this."

"Absolutely. Is it really so unbelievable? We live in a time when men can fly through the air to drop bombs on each other, when invisible rays allow us to photograph people's skeletons, and when other rays allow us to talk to people miles away. Why is it so impossible that there might be other rays that turn men's thoughts into actions?"

"But. . . all right, I'm as firm a believer in the occult as anyone. If you say rituals can have effects on the material plane, and not just the spiritual, then I'll believe you. But I have to say I find it absolutely flabbergasting. I mean – couldn't this have serious military potential? Why aren't we using it?"

"What on Earth makes you think we aren't?"

"What?"

"Why do you think I know all of this stuff? It's not for my own entertainment – believe me, I find many of the degenerates who practice this magic utterly repulsive. It's because we in the Service need to know these things in order to use them."

Driberg took out his cigarette case, and again he offered a cigarette to Knight, who again shook his head. Driberg lit one, and started puffing clouds of ghastly-smelling smoke in

Knight's direction. Cheap cigarettes, thought Knight, for a fundamentally cheap man. Driberg shook the match to put it out, and dropped it in the ashtray on Knight's desk.

"But I assume we haven't any practitioners who can actually manifest stuff on the physical plane?"

"You may assume that if you wish, yes."

Driberg took another puff of his cigarette, while considering the implications of the answer. "All right. Do we have anyone who could perform a ritual to counter this?"

"On that, at least, I can give you a simple answer. We have nobody who has the power to defeat this ritual. I don't even know of anyone who might be able to. Well, apart from one man..."

Chapter 26

There are few things in the world that seem darker than a graveyard at midnight, in a time of war when blackouts mean that not a single light is visible anywhere. As Ian Fleming and Dennis Wheatley approached the church, the whole world seemed still and quiet, as if the whole of creation was engulfed in silence.

There was nothing moving anywhere, and the shielded lamp that Wheatley carried, with its tiny flicker of light just barely enough to allow them to see three feet ahead of them, gave those few shrubs and tufts of grass that were visible a spectral pallor which, along with the musty smell coming up from the muddy ground, made it seem like at any moment the dead bodies around them could rise up from their rest and rejoin the living world.

Even in darkness, though, it can still be advisable to find a hiding place from which to observe people, should the people one wishes to observe not be in the mood for such observations. The two men found a suitable bush to crouch behind, with a wall behind them to prevent anyone coming up from the rear.

They sat there for ten minutes, waiting for their eyes to adjust to the night, and Fleming mused on all the things that had had to go wrong to get them to this stage. His plan had been so reasonable, and had worked so well at first, that it was almost impossible to see how he'd managed to get from the great success of Hess actually taking the bait to the ultimate loss of Turing being at risk of sacrifice.

To take his mind off his own failures, Fleming decided to try to poke a weak spot in his companion's activities, in case he could find him to blame for everything somehow.

"So you're *sure* this is the place?" he whispered to Wheatley, "I haven't seen anyone coming this way yet."

"I have it from the most reliable source imaginable," Wheatley replied, *sotto voce*. "Just wait. They'll be here soon enough."

They saw cars pulling up and several men going in, but it was too dark to see their faces from where Fleming and Wheatley were positioned, though they made note of the license plate numbers for later research.

"Damn blackout. Wish we could get a decent look at who they are."

"I'd say that turning up to a deconsecrated church at midnight is, by itself, *prima facie* evidence of wrongdoing of some kind."

"Indeed. Clandestine meetings of this type are precisely the sort of thing we need to be monitoring."

Wheatley shushed Fleming and pointed. In the distance, they saw two figures walking toward them – the silhouettes of a short, healthy, man helping an older, frailer, man along the road. As the figures became clearer, what had been obvious to Wheatley became apparent too to Fleming – it was Crowley, being helped to the church by Turing. The two men were talking, too quietly for Fleming to hear.

When the two men had entered, Fleming turned to Wheatley.

"We've got to do something! Alan's in serious danger, and he doesn't even realise it! It's like Crowley has put a glamour on him, and he's possessed now."

"He very well may be. We must assess the situation carefully. We have a little time left. They won't do anything until dawn tomorrow."

He was obviously going to be held there until the sacrifice

in thirty-six hours' time. They had to get Turing out of there, and stop the hideous ritual from taking place.

The two men continued to wait in silence, occasionally glancing at their watches. Fleming wished that the church clock had still been in use – it was almost impossible to see anything on the watch face in this blackness – but that line of thought was closed off by another thought altogether.

"Dennis?"

"What?"

"I've just thought. . ."

Fleming's thought was interrupted by the sound of bells chiming, coming from within the church.

"What the *hell* is going on?" Fleming yelled, no longer keeping his voice down as any sound would be drowned out by the bells anyway. "I thought that church was out of use?"

"Clearly the bells remain in working order."

Eventually, the bell-ringing stopped. In any other part of the world the noise would have attracted attention, but evidently the good people of Torquay were not the kind of people to go investigating strange goings-on in abandoned churches, and Fleming was beginning to see the advantages of such a lack of curiosity.

Once Fleming was certain that the bell-ringing had stopped, he returned to his previous line of conversation. "I've just thought – what if Alan isn't the sacrifice? What if he has willingly gone over to the Nazis' side?"

"Do you really think so little of your young friend?"

"Of course not! It's just. . ."

"I know. You can never truly trust anyone. But if I'm any judge of character, and I like to believe I am, young Alan is as sound a man as you're going to find. I don't think for one moment that he would betray his country, and certainly not into the hands of someone as foul as Crowley."

Fleming got up and stretched. His entire body was cramping up from having to stay in a crouching position on such a cold, damp, night. Even though it was now summer, the nights were still fiercely cold, and Fleming wondered how Wheatley was managing to cope with the discomfort. But then, Wheatley had served in the last war, so he was probably used to worse.

Fleming looked down at his old friend, and saw that Wheatley was actually grinning to himself.

"What's so damn funny, Dennis?"

"Oh, nothing. Nothing much. Just thought how this would look to any of my readers. Like I've started believing in my own stories. But the Duc de Richelieu never felt so bloody terrified as this."

Fleming nodded. Wheatley seemed calm to Fleming, compared to his own feelings, but Fleming had no doubt that the older man was just hiding his feelings better.

Stuck in that dark graveyard, with who knew what monstrosity taking place mere yards away, only a fool would not have been terrified.

Chapter 27

Now that they knew where Turing was being held, the next step was to ensure that they could defeat any of the forces that Crowley could mass against them. Wheatley explained it to Fleming.

"I am, of course, a Pagan, and have no more belief in the Christian God than I have in Father Christmas or the innate goodness of mankind. Does this bother you?"

"My dear fellow, if I was upset by people holding differing opinions from my own, I could not serve in Naval Intelligence. I have found that every man has his own politics, and his own religion, and that even when we say 'I am a Conservative' or 'I am a Christian', it does not mean the same as when the next fellow says it."

"Good. So are you willing to take part in a ritual – a Christian ritual – with me, even though I am a nonbeliever?"

"That depends entirely on what the ritual is for."

"It is to keep us safe from Crowley's evil magicks. The man is on the side of darkness – of Moloch, and of Baal, and of filth and destruction. The dark side cannot stand against the light, once the light is turned upon it."

Wheatley pulled out two crucifixes from his pockets, and handed one to Fleming, while putting the other on himself.

"I know many consider the crucifix idolatrous, but symbols have their own power, This symbol is the antithesis of everything for which Crowley stands. It may well offer more protection than anything else could."

Once he had the crucifix fastened around his neck, Wheatley held the cross to his lips and kissed it reverently, and gestured to Fleming to do the same.

"Whatever your own beliefs – and I don't need to know them – we're on England's soil now, and England is a Christian nation. Not only that, but the ground we are standing on, while deconsecrated, was once hallowed ground, and that protection can never truly be removed. The symbol of the Holy Cross is the most potent symbol of them all, in this place, in this time."

Wheatley kneeled on the stony ground, rucking his trousers at the knee to avoid creasing them as he knelt, and Fleming did likewise. Wheatley's voice, while whispered, still sounded resonant, as if his words themselves carried a power.

"Oh Lord, protect us thy servants from the iniquities of the evil one, and from all the forces of the dark he has at his command. Let us walk like Daniel into the lions' den, and we shall fear no evil, for thou art with us.

"Now repeat after me: 'Our father, which art in heaven, hallowed be thy name...'"

The two men repeated the Lord's Prayer, hoping for its efficacy even though neither was a traditional believer. Both had said those words so many times, at school and in church growing up, that they were burned into their souls.

Still, Fleming had not thought about the words much before. As a prayer, it seemed to encompass a lot more than he had remembered – it covered the spiritual and physical worlds, and was a concrete list of things to be done. It was a practical list, from a practical time, assuming one believed at all in a higher power and the world of the spirit. But it was the phrase near the end, "deliver us from evil", which mattered most that night.

They would need that delivery, for the place they were going to enter was possibly the most evil place in Britain at that time. Fleming didn't know what had convinced him – maybe just the location and the time, maybe the older man's conviction – but he was absolutely sure now that devilry *was* happening at that church. He was as sure of it as he was of his own name.

For there was something evil in the air around that church. It wasn't just the darkness, or the faint mist, that was giving the graveyard the unholy atmosphere. This was not just a church that had been deconsecrated, but one that seemed to be fighting against the very idea of holiness. Merely speaking the Lord's Prayer was difficult in these surroundings.

The prayer ended, and Fleming gave the most heartfelt "Amen" of his life. He was unsure whether he believed in the personal God to whom he had prayed, but he was sure that if there were a Devil at work among the lives of men, then there must be some equal and opposite spirit of goodness, and to that spirit he entrusted his own wellbeing.

"Before the final preparations," Wheatley asked, "is there anything on your conscience which you wish to repent? Anything that gives you unease about the destination of your soul?"

Fleming thought very carefully for a short while. "No," he finally replied, "I don't think so. I've done many things of which I'm not proud, of course, but nothing for which I don't think I could account to my maker. Nothing without good cause."

They sprinkled themselves with holy water, and went through the ritual of extreme unction in case of their death.

"I pray we shall not need these rites, and that we shall return from this adventure unharmed both physically and spiritually," said Wheatley, "but while our spiritual health is protected by our prayers, our physical health is not. There is a very strong chance we shall die, and I hope that this at least will prevent our souls being taken by he whom we fight."

Fleming shuddered, and then braced himself. "All right. This is it. We have to go and face the traitors, no matter what the cost to ourselves."

The two men pulled out their revolvers and crept towards the church doors, trying to give those inside as little notice as possible of their entrance. Fleming took hold of one of the giant brass-ring doorknobs, and gently turned it. Once he was sure the door was unlocked, he whispered "three, two, one..." under his breath, and then the two men burst into the church, pistols drawn.

"Get down!" Fleming shouted, but then he took in the sight in front of them. There in the pews, along with Crowley and Turing, sat Tom Driberg and Maxwell Knight.

Chapter 28

Both groups of men stood, open-mouthed and unspeaking, for several seconds, gazing in silent shock at each other. Something, somewhere, had obviously gone very, very, wrong, and none of them were quite sure what that could possibly be.

Fleming gazed around the church, taking in the stained glass windows, the pews, the hymnals – left there despite the church's disuse, and now mildewed, but still recognisable – and the faint smell of candles and incense, presumably there from Crowley's unholy rituals rather than the more wholesome practices of the Church of England. And most of all, he took in the sight of his colleagues, clearly in league with the Satanic Crowley himself.

What could possibly have caused this? How could people he'd trusted, people whom the *British Empire* had trusted, to defeat the German menace, have become so utterly lost as to be willing to work with an actual Satan-worshipper? How could they have gone over to the dark side? How high did the corruption go? Were the Prime Minister or the King himself secretly Satanists? Suddenly nothing seemed impossible.

Maxwell Knight, the most senior member of the intelligence services present and thus to all intents and purposes the leader of both groups, was the first to speak, and he directed his horror at the interruption squarely at his old friend Wheatley.

"Dennis, what the hell are you doing?"

"I might ask you the same question, Max. I thought that you were on the *British* side. I knew you were friends with

Crowley of course, but I never for one moment thought you'd be a traitor."

"Traitor? What on Earth are you blithering about man? I'm trying to have a discussion with my friends here and you come bursting in brandishing a crucifix like you're in a Boris Karloff film. Speak, man! What are you playing at?"

Wheatley stammered for a second, and then regained his composure.

"What I'm playing at is trying to save Mr. Turing there from being sacrificed to Satan."

Crowley laughed loud and heartily, until Knight glared at him, at which point he started snorting under his breath instead.

"Satan?" Knight said, with audible contempt. "Dennis, you're confusing real life with one of your own potboilers. Think like an adult, man!"

Fleming, having been silent up until this point, thought that he had better engage in at least a half-hearted defence of his friend.

"We thought. . ."

"You thought what, exactly?"

Fleming straightened his posture. If this was going to be an inquisition, he would do better if he kept a military bearing.

Knight explained to the intruders that the group were actually discussing what could be done to *disrupt* the Nazi occultists. Crowley was on the side of the angels, at least on this occasion. Wheatley grudgingly apologised.

Turing spent much of the rest of the meeting trying to hold back a snigger, as Knight berated Wheatley and Ian Fleming for their incompetence and idiocy.

"You could easily have blown the whole thing, you stupid, stupid buggers! What could possibly have possessed you to traipse all the way down to Torquay and to sneak around like a couple of schoolboys trying to steal biscuits from the headmaster's study? What on Earth did you think you were going to achieve by that?"

"Well, we thought that Alan was going to be sacrificed to the Devil."

"Oh did you now? And I suppose you also thought that Mickey Mouse was going to be performing the sacrifice, and Billy Bunter would be drinking his blood afterwards? Are you a *child*? Such things just don't happen in Britain!"

"Sir Maxwell, we were proceeding on the basis of the best information available to us. Perhaps had you deigned to inform us. . ."

"*Inform* you? You utter arse, Fleming, *you* are meant to provide information to *me*, not the other way round, and *I* am then to give you your orders. What on Earth you thought you were doing running off half-cocked like that. . ."

Crowley stood up, and at his commanding presence Knight immediately fell silent.

Crowley seemed, to Fleming at least, much taller than he had appeared previously. It was almost as if he could make himself grow or shrink to fit the situation, and now he positively towered above the other men, his bald head and glowering, bushy, eyebrows making him the picture of authority.

"As fascinating as I find your dispute over the chain of command in His Supposed Majesty's Intelligence Services, I have to say that I would find it even more fascinating if we could perhaps discuss what we are to do about the situation in which we find ourselves."

The men murmured their assent, and Crowley continued. "The problem we have before us is a simple one. A rite is to be performed in a matter of hours. Because of your buffoonery, we have no idea where or by whom, but we know that it is a rite which may bring about the downfall of Britain and her Empire. Is that a reasonable summary of matters as they stand?"

Knight nodded, while Fleming and Wheatley looked on resentfully.

"As I thought. We must therefore now pool our information, if we wish to have any hope at all of succeeding. What, exactly, do we know, and how do we know it?"

Driberg went first. "Well, for a start, I know for sure that Lord Keynsham is involved in this mess. He's the leader of the band who kidnapped me."

"Good," replied Crowley. "That is one actual piece of information we can use. What else do we know? Facts, not suppositions, not hypotheses and speculation."

"Well," said Turing, "we do know what ritual they're planning to perform, even if we're unsure of what exactly it's meant to accomplish."

Crowley's eyes widened.

"Well, why on Earth did you not say so? That changes everything. I am more than capable of ascertaining the intended results of any ritual with which I am presented. The rules of magick are simple ones, and are susceptible to scientific analysis just as any other actions are. Tell me what the plan is."

Chapter 29

Driberg perched himself at the edge of one of the pews, leaned an elbow against the back of the pew in front, and with his other arm pulled his cigarette case from his inside jacket pocket. He took out a cigarette, tapped it on the case, and put the case back in his pocket. He took out a packet of matches, struck one against the pew back, and lit the cigarette, which immediately filled the air with a foul-smelling odour. Wheatley nodded to himself – Driberg was a man with no real taste, after all, for all his pretended sophistication.

After going through this ritual, as formal and stylised in its way as the one through which Wheatley had earlier guided Fleming, Driberg finally got down to business.

"Do you know much about Keynsham?" he asked Wheatley.

"Not really, I've seen him mentioned in the papers occasionally, but I haven't paid him much attention. He's the one with the ridiculous hair?"

"That's right. He's also an occultist, and a Nazi sympathiser. And I am convinced he's the one behind all of this. He's a loon of course, and he has no real understanding of how the world actually works. But he's the kind of loon whose views make a kind of sense with each other – there's a logic there of a sort. Once you accept the premises, everything else does follow."

"So tell me about this Keynsham fellow."

"Well, Ian knows quite a bit about him, as it happens."

"Yes, we've been keeping tabs on him for quite some time. Rum fellow, not someone I'd trust as far as I could throw him."

Fleming explained that Keynsham was a true obsessive on the subject of Bolshevism, and that he considered all other subjects, even the survival of the Empire itself, as of secondary importance to that subject. He'd advocated alliance with Nazi Germany right up to the point hostilities broke out, and even afterwards had proposed increasingly unlikely peace plans.

"He's full of strange ideas. He wants to restore Edward to the throne – calls the King a usurper, though he hasn't made as much of that since the war started. And he wants England to have dominion over Scotland. Says he doesn't believe in the concept of the United Kingdom, but in English supremacy. Listening to one of his speeches is like reading a Bulwer-Lytton novel rewritten by Austen Chamberlain."

Wheatley was still confused. "But I thought the man was a patriot? I'd have thought him incapable of treachery. Idiocy, bone-idleness, and drunkenness, yes, but not actually giving his country up to a foreign power."

Fleming nodded. "True. But you see, he doesn't think he is. He thinks he's saving England from the threat of Communism."

"Is the man absolutely mad?"

"Oh, no doubt about it. The plan makes absolutely no kind of sense, and has no chance of working. Even if the ritual itself worked – which I sincerely doubt – the idea that the country will suddenly ally with the people who've spent the last eighteen months dropping bombs on us is imbecilic."

"Not only that, but the Nazis and the bloody bolshies are two sides of the same coin anyway! Hasn't he heard of the Molotov-Ribbentrop pact?" Wheatley asked.

"He has, but he thinks the Nazis are being deceived about the Soviets' intentions." Fleming replied.

"Clue's in the name. National *Socialists.*"

Turing laughed. "Oh come on, Dennis, you don't really think that because they use the word 'socialist' in their name they're actually socialists? They're not exactly the Labour Party, you know."

"Oh no?"

"No of course not!"

"Then why was Moseley a Labour man before he formed his own party?"

Driberg smiled. "I'm in Labour myself, you know."

Wheatley was unabashed. "Always knew there was something fishy about you."

Driberg started to redden, and Fleming began to fear that the group were going to fall apart before they could even get started on the job at hand, over political arguments. Wheatley being a high Tory and Driberg being... whatever he was, something Fleming had never properly understood... they were never going to get on. Thankfully, Crowley interrupted before the discussion turned more acrimonious.

"The ideological differences between Comrade Stalin and Herr Hitler are hardly germane to our present discussion," said Crowley. "Perhaps rather than discussing which particular dictator you would prefer to kneel before, we should instead concentrate our efforts on preventing either man, however admirable, from conquering England?"

Turing nodded. "Yes, we shan't stop this by nattering about politics."

"Indeed," said Crowley. "Whether the Nazis and the Bolsheviks are in agreement or dispute, or whether both are being controlled by some secret third party, we know at least that Keynsham believes them to be allied. Whether he is delusional is of less interest than in what direction his beliefs, delusional or otherwise, will lead him."

"And those beliefs," Wheatley said, "are clearly leading him to try to destroy the whole of the British Empire. Do you think there's any chance at all he will succeed?"

"Oh, from what you've told me I'm quite certain he will," replied Crowley. "The question is, do you want him to?"

"I beg your pardon?" exclaimed Fleming. "Are you seriously suggesting we should want the British Empire destroyed? I thought you'd said you were on *our* side?"

Crowley smiled. "Oh, I most definitely am. But the British Empire will be gone in a generation, no matter what actions we take today. The question is merely whether you wish it to collapse from rot or be swept away in a glorious fire. But I see from your expressions you all prefer the former. I shall ask no further."

The other men all appeared to want to interject, but Crowley continued, not allowing them a chance to speak.

"So, we have a magickal ritual to defeat, then. I must say our chances are small, but we must do what we can. Before we begin our counterattack, I shall need to know everything that is known about this Lord Keynsham. I must know our enemy."

Chapter 30

The Robing room in the Palace of Westminster is traditionally used by the monarch for donning the robes of state before the opening of Parliament. However, as the Commons chamber had been bombed, it now had a new use. While the MPs used the Lords' chamber for their debates, the Lords in turn used the Robing room.

And so the Lords temporal and spiritual sat, in a room designed for a monarch to change from his private to his public appearance, and listened to a man whose whole persona was a public facade, as he talked about how to defeat Satan while in fact embracing him entirely.

Or at least, some of the Lords temporal and spiritual sat there. There is no constitutional, moral, or legal imperative for Peers to attend Parliament at all, and many never turn up from one year to the next. Others will turn up merely to collect their attendance allowance, eat a good meal subsidised by the British taxpayer, and leave again.

But even that minority of Lords who take their service seriously, who regularly attend debates and regard their privilege as a sacred responsibility to their country, are not obliged to sit through every windy interjection from their fellows, and when certain peers get up to speak, many take that as a signal to retire temporarily.

So, as was so often the case when Lord Keynsham spoke, the chamber was largely empty. And as was so often the case,

Keynsham didn't seem to notice this.

The debate had been going on most of the night, and most of the Lords had already left, to retire to bed. Keynsham was also soon to leave, though in his case to make a journey in the direction of his ancestral seat. But he had time yet before he needed to depart, and he had something to say.

Lord Keynsham was once again on his favourite hobbyhorse, talking about how the Communists were tools of the Devil, and how Stalin was Lucifer himself, raised from Hell and attempting to start the final war between good and evil foretold in the Revelation of St. John the Divine. Most of the Lords were either sleeping or staring in silent fury at their colleague, whose increasing obsession with the need to destroy Bolshevism was taking valuable time away from the real work of Parliament.

At one end of the chamber stood an enormous fireplace, made of multicoloured marble from all over Great Britain and Ireland. Flanking it were two bronze statuettes – one of St. George and the dragon, and the other, to which Keynsham's eyes kept turning, of Saint Michael the Archangel vanquishing Satan.

While his mop of white hair and bumbling manner gave the impression of affable idiocy, most who knew Keynsham saw him as a great, though deeply misguided, intellect – a Machiavellian manipulator who could never safely be underestimated. "A backstabbing, vicious, nasty little spiv" was the description used by one of his closest friends.

"These people are, let us remember, monsters. They are regicides, and are in the control of demonic forces. They claim neutrality in the current conflict, but make no mistake, they are the true power behind Hitler. When Ribbentrop signed the pact with the red filth, he signed away Germany's soul."

How Keynsham squared this belief with his own involvement with Satanists is perhaps a question the attentive reader will be asking, and so a digression into the history of Gnosticism is necessary. Keynsham believed, as many so-called Satanists have over the years, that the creator of the world and the God of the Christian Bible are two different entities.

For many dabblers in the esoteric side of Christianity, it seems obvious that the physical and spiritual worlds are the work of two very different entities – and that the fallen physical world is created by a demiurge, not the real god, whose emanation is pure light. Prometheus, bringer of fire to mortals; Lucifer, the light bearer, these are the figures of mythology and creation which the more mystical Satanists identified as the true creative force of the universe.

Keynsham, then, saw Christians as being fundamentally confused about the identities of God and the Devil, but he also saw materialism itself as being the true evil – and both the Nazi and Soviet worldviews were fundamentally materialist dogmas. To Keynsham, they were concerned with perfecting the physical world. He wanted to see it destroyed altogether.

Keynsham believed that the big threat to Britain was Communism, and wanted to restore Edward VIII to the throne (even though Edward was the descendant of the Norman conquerors – the "Saxon restoration" was not the intended end of the ritual, just a way of turning the spirit of England against its current rulers) and make peace with Germany. The ritual he had planned would help bring this about, after which Keynsham would be made dictator under Edward's rule, ally with Germany, and go to war with the USSR.

As the few Lords still bothering to listen to his speech started to grow angry, Keynsham quickly continued, "and so I say to Comrade Stalin, exactly as I say to Herr Hitler – you shall be destroyed by the righteous fire of the British Empire. We shall destroy all traces of the Bolshevik menace, and restore the world to its rightful glory."

And in saying this, at least, Keynsham was entirely honest. He was, in his own way, a sincere, passionate, idealist – it was merely that the ideals for which he stood were not ones that the rest of the population could recognise even as coherent statements, much less as ideals worth dying for.

But to Keynsham, those ideals were certainly worth as many deaths as it took, so long as one of those deaths was not his own.

And he was certain it would not be. For was his cause not righteous? Was his arm not strong? Was the defeat of the Bolshevik menace and the restoration of the Angelcynn to their proper position of supremacy over the lesser races not a cause which the gods themselves had ordained? No, he would not die. But many others would.

He regretted it, but such things are the price of righteousness.

Chapter 31

"Well, this is a bloody pickle, isn't it? We thought Alan was infiltrating the Nazis, and instead we've wasted all this effort infiltrating our own side."

"Well maybe," replied Knight, "if you'd bothered talking with me before running off half-cocked and coming up with your own ridiculous plans, this wouldn't have happened."

Wheatley and Fleming looked at each other. Knight was clearly correct, but at the same time it wasn't something either man would like to admit. The truth was, this *shouldn't* have happened – but they also didn't have any better leads than the ones they'd followed. They had been so convinced that Crowley was involved that they hadn't considered what to do if they were wrong.

They shivered, and neither man was sure whether it was because of the chill in the unheated church or the thought of the fate to which they had nearly consigned the British Empire, and which it might yet meet were they not to defeat the occult forces which were massed against it.

With no-one now inside the organisation, they were left with a problem – they didn't have any clue where the ritual was to be carried out.

"Have any of you any ideas at all? Crowley?"

Crowley shifted in his seat, and an air of superiority crept over his face. "Well, of course, I have *ideas*. The problem is not with a lack of ideas on my part, but with a lack of knowledge of the depths of our adversaries' ignorance."

"How do you mean?"

"Well, quite simply, there are places in the country that are more susceptible to magickal influence than others. Some of these places are very well known, and even *hoi polloi* understand that those places are holy, or enchanted. Others, however – often the most powerful – are not major landmarks or tourist spots. Some of the most magickal places keep their natures hidden. The single most powerful place I know of is the outhouse attached to a bungalow owned by a dear old lady in Aberdeen, who has no more knowledge of its power than an ant has of the tactics being used on the African front. What we need to discover is how many of these places are within our opponents' knowledge."

"And how do you intend to do that?" Fleming asked, still unconvinced that Crowley wasn't just bluffing.

"Well, I shall have to ask them, shan't I?"

Wheatley was by now openly contemptuous. "So you expect to go up to these people – people whose identity we don't even know, incidentally – and just say to them 'excuse me, sir, but would you mind telling me exactly where your ritual to destroy the British Empire will be taking place?' You don't see any kind of flaw in that plan?"

Crowley sneered. "Of course I 'see any kind of flaw in that plan'." Wheatley's face reddened at the imitation of his voice, all the more insulting for its accuracy. "Which is why I intend to ask them *on the astral plane*, where only the greatest of magi – such as myself – can keep secrets at all."

Turing's interest was suddenly piqued.

"You mean to tell us, Sir Aleister, that on the astral plane an adept can communicate with complete secrecy, through a channel that cannot be intercepted, but can also retrieve the most secret data from the minds of his enemies without detection?"

Crowley looked nonplussed. "I suppose that would be one way of looking at things, yes, although that does rather reduce the nature of the spiritual experience to that of some kind of telephone."

"Do you not see what that would mean for communications during wartime? An agent could communicate without need for ciphers or codebooks. It would make the risk of capture almost non-existent, and also avoid the possibility of fraudulent signals. It would absolutely revolutionise the art of espionage!"

"I am not at all sure that such a revolution would be desirable," interrupted Knight. "Perfect security is a defence which destroys the possibility of offence."

Turing smiled. "Oh, it would not be perfect security. There can be no such thing. It would merely require the players of the game to grow more sophisticated in their techniques. Attempting to decrypt communications one cannot even detect, made through an unbreakable channel. . . that would be an interesting problem all right."

"It would indeed," said Crowley, "and I should be most interested in discussing your thoughts on the matter at some point in the future – assuming, that is, that we have a future. But at the present moment I must ask you to refrain from speech, while I assume my *asana* and allow my spirit to depart from my body and perform the reconnaissance we require."

Crowley stood, then slowly stretched out his arms, extending them to the sky. He then let his right arm fall to his side, while he touched his left index finger to the tip of his nose. He lifted his right leg, and bent the knee at ninety degrees, rolled his eyes back in his head, and started to let out a slow, repetitive moan. And his spirit started to perceive things more clearly.

Blue stones. Warm air. The astral *plain*, all of England's history converging at one point. And yes, it's *England*'s history. This isn't anything to do with Britain – although the stones are Welsh – it's an English war, a deep cleft at the heart of England itself finally causing a snapping in two.

The split, between the East and the West. Keynsham a West Country man, a *country* man, not one for the city.

City sophistication, cosmopolitanism, these were the things to be destroyed. Feudalism and forelock-tugging peasants. Or no. . . something even older than that. Something darker. A return to truly dark ages, pre-Roman. To blue-painted savagery.

Mistletoe. A winter flower, but it was going to play a part. Symbol of death and rebirth, of the dying and resurrecting god. They were going to bring something back – a spirit long thought banished. A spirit of blood sacrifice and vengeance, of long dark nights and short cold days. A spirit of pagan England barely visible in the modern palimpsest Great Britain.

"They're going to do it at Stonehenge."

Chapter 32

The distance from Torquay to Stonehenge is a little over a hundred miles, and every yard of that hundred mile journey seemed like a mile in itself. Crowley, Turing, Knight, and Wheatley in one car, and Driberg and Fleming in another, were attempting to get to Stonehenge as quickly as possible, but at every turn everything that could possibly go wrong did.

Engines overheated, tyres were punctured, roads were mysteriously flooded even though it was the middle of June, and the maps they were using seemed to include roads which were not visible in the physical world through which they were travelling.

Knight was convinced that this was all evidence of the conspiracy against them. "Keynsham's using his psychic forces against us"

"Nonsense," replied Crowley. "The man has no psychic power to speak of. He's an amateur, a dilettante. He has merely called up a greater power, which he is attempting to use for his own ends. But that power will destroy him. Have no doubt of that."

"Jesus Christ!"

Wheatley yelled as his car suddenly threw itself into reverse. He grabbed hold of the wheel and tried desperately to turn it round. The steering wheel wouldn't move, so he grabbed the handbrake and yanked it as hard as he could. The car started to skid, and Wheatley used all his strength to turn the steering wheel. He managed, just, to manoeuvre the car to the side of the road before it came to a halt.

Had the roads not been so empty as a result of petrol rationing, they would have undoubtedly died.

Wheatley sat at the driver's seat for several seconds, trembling and pale, before slowly unclenching the fists that were wrapped around the steering wheel. He turned, shaking, to look at the others.

"Is everybody unharmed?"

Turing and Crowley looked at each other and nodded.

"No physical harm has been incurred," said Crowley, "while my own spiritual state is resilient enough. Mr. Turing?"

"Oh, I've been in worse scrapes than that. What happened, Dennis? Doesn't seem the weather for black ice."

"That's just the thing. Nothing happened. The car itself seemed to take control." Wheatley turned angrily towards Crowley. "And you say Keynsham has no psychic power? He has enough to nearly get us killed!"

"A parlour trick, that's all. Like I say, the man's a dilettante. Should a real adept have wanted to kill us, make no mistake, we should be dead."

They got out of the car, and watched as the car containing Fleming and Driberg met a similar fate. There was no doubt now, this wasn't just a simple mechanical failure, but a symptom of attack by a malevolent magical force far greater than any in their previous experience.

There seemed to be some sort of invisible barrier. Further experimentation, over the course of an hour or more, suggested that it was possible for them to pass through the barrier on foot, but that any attempt to drive through it would be met with the same resistance. Turing did some quick calculations, using the map and a pair of compasses.

"The curve seems to suggest a circle, maybe twenty miles in radius. It seems to be centred on Stonehenge, so Crowley was probably right that that's where they're going to do it. We can keep trying with the cars, of course, but I suspect we're not going to get any further."

They decided to split up. Wheatley, Turing, and Fleming would attempt to get there physically, while Knight, Crowley, and Driberg would attack on the astral plane.

"It would make sense," Crowley said, "for those of us practiced in the arts of magick to work on the higher levels, while those of you who have no such experience will deal with mere matter."

"Mere matter can be fairly important," replied Fleming. "I should certainly not wish to live in a world which lacked the pleasures of the flesh, and nor I think would you."

Crowley smiled. "The flesh does have its attractions – why else should I have tarried so long in this body, rather than take on my true form? – but when dealing with those entities which shape our destinies, it is naught but an encumbrance, and must be discarded at least for the moment."

"How do you mean, discarded?" asked Turing.

"You will be aware, I am sure, of Herr Einstein's discovery that matter is merely another form of energy, and that neither can travel at a speed faster than that of light? Herr Einstein is mistaken in one crucial matter. That form of energy which we call spirit is not bounded by that or any other limit."

Turing laughed. "Sometimes I actually believe in this occult nonsense you peddle, but then you come out with something like that, and I'm more convinced than ever that you don't actually understand the scientific justifications you provide at all. If you understood relativity at all, you'd understand why everything you said is unmitigated bunkum."

"And if you, my young friend, understood the lessons of the great occultists throughout the ages, you in turn would understand that relativity is merely an application of principles which were known long before Herr Einstein made his discovery – and a woefully incomplete application, at that, which misses many of the most important points."

Turing shook his head, smiling. But he supposed it wasn't

his concern what nonsense his temporary colleague chose to believe. And Turing had, of course, held similar delusions himself while growing up. It was more important to get the job done than to continue the eternal argument over superstition and rationalism.

"Anyway," Crowley continued, "as I was saying before, I believe that those of us with experience of the magickal arts must take the battle to the astral plane, while those of you whose skills lie elsewhere should continue on foot. We shall need both physical and spiritual success if we are to thwart these plans — success on one plane of reality will not be enough."

Driberg and Knight nodded, their faces tense. While their companions were going to face mortal peril, Driberg, Knight, and Crowley were going to risk their very immortal souls.

Chapter 33

As soon as Wheatley, Turing, and Fleming had left, Crowley's expression and posture changed dramatically.

"Now that they're out of the way, we can do the real work. They have little chance of doing anything worthwhile to disrupt the sacrifice, but we can't have cowans watching while we perform the Great Work, can we?"

He bent down to the ground, and started drawing symbols in the dirt with his finger.

"You may remember the story of Yeheshua ben Yusuf, vulgarly called Jesus Christ, and the adulteress. She was to be stoned to death, and ben Yusuf prevented the crowd from their attacks. The part of the story that most remember is his phrase 'let he who is without sin cast the first stone', but that would of course not by itself have had the desired effect, as those like myself whose souls are spotless could still have been willing and able to kill her.

"The part of the story that most of the uninitiated forget is that, before speaking, he knelt and wrote in the dust. The Bible, of course, does not say what it was he wrote, and so like most of the mysteries in that book those who claim to believe in its inerrance simply dismiss it without thinking about it.

"But what he was writing was, of course, the only part of the story that is of any interest whatsoever, and is encoded kabbalistically in the story itself, for those who know how to look. These symbols I am writing now are the same ones written by Yeheshua then. Written correctly, they can prevent any physical harm whatsoever."

Crowley finished his writing, and Driberg looked down and laughed out loud.

"I used to draw things like that on the blackboard at school!"

Crowley looked at Driberg with utter contempt. "No doubt you did. But you should know better than most that a fool and an apostle can look at the same mirror and see only themselves reflected in it. The same goes for these holiest of symbols."

"Really? You're serious? *That* is what was drawn by Christ?"

"I am always serious. Your Christ was, after all, a holy man. He was in many ways a genius, and he was certainly as aware as anyone of the power of the generative spirit."

Knight nodded. "I should have thought that you would have understood yourself, Tom. It is rather a subject on which you are expert."

Crowley ascended to the astral, where he saw Hess' spirit, now outside his body, guiding a more malignant force towards Stonehenge.

The spirit was definitely that of Hess – Crowley could recognise it instantly. The man had so little imagination, so little natural talent for magick, that his god-form was almost indistinguishable from his mortal body. Crowley could feel nothing but utter contempt for anyone so thoroughly mundane, and he decided that Hess should be no concern to him. The other force, though, was a different matter.

That force, Crowley was certain, was something utterly inimical to human life. There were inhabitants of the higher planes whose attitudes towards humanity were friendly, and those who were contemptuous or oblivious. But this one was something else. This being was anti-human, an entity whose highest ambition was to rid the world of those things humans valued.

Crowley invoked the god Horus, the conquering child-god.

"Io Hoor, Io Hoor, Io Io!"

"Io Heru-ra-ha! Io Ra-Hoor-Khuit! Io Hoor-paar-kraat! Io! Io!"

In a five-sided pentagon of fire, the crowned and conquering child, the warrior lord of the forties, the Lord of the Aeon, appeared.

Horus, the hawk-headed god of war, here in his incarnation as Harpocrates, the silent child god of dawn and new beginnings.

The gods are not visible with normal human eyes – they are manifestations of ideas, from a higher set of dimensions. To them we appear as paper cut-out figures, moving through tissue-thin lives of an unimaginable fragility, while to us they have multiple simultaneous aspects, each more fearsome than the others.From one angle, he looked like a giggling mad child smashing things for his own amusement, from another, a wise man, older than time, keeping his own counsel. And from a third, he appeared as a vengeful bird of prey, out to devour everything in its path. On his forehead, his hand, and his heart, appeared a symbol combining the sun and moon. He turned toward Hess, and screeched.

Hess' spirit recoiled in terror from the apparition, but found himself surrounded by Horus' talons. Try as he might, he could not escape from the vengeful god – there is no escape from an idea, once it has taken root in your mind, and Hess' occult practices had rendered him susceptible to Horus' power.

Horus crushed Hess with the realisation of what he'd really been working for. Hess screamed, as he understood for the first time what death really meant, and the incalculable obscenity of the millions of deaths his leader had caused in pursuit of his dream. He understood now that what he had considered nobility was instead devastation and destruction. His mind screamed, unable to comprehend the enormity of his actions, and shattered into a million screaming fragments.

Hess' spirit returned, broken, to his body. He was too fractured, now, to ever again achieve the mental unity and concentration necessary to perform magick. The man who had been called Rudolf Hess, indeed, no longer existed. What had taken his place was a mere fragment of a man, nothing more than an obedient puppet who would act under the sway of any influence.

"Do you think it was a good idea to let him go? With everything he now knows about the war effort?"

"Driberg, you always were a pusillanimous coward," replied Crowley. "Had you half the spirit of your Communist heroes, you would by now be a power to rival the gods, rather than a scribbler of infantile columns under a pseudonym."

The wind gained strength, as if the forces of nature were massing against the occultists. "The easy part is over," said Crowley, "but the real fight starts now. We must ascend to the astral, to assist Ra-Hoor-Khuit in his destruction of our enemies. We must abandon the physical plane, and take flight."

Chapter 34

Stonehenge is the oldest known place of worship in Britain, dating back more than five thousand years. But as long as there has been worship there, there has also been death. Stonehenge was a burial ground – and perhaps a site for sacrifice – from the time it was created. The bluestones are built on bones.

There is a tale that the stones were brought to Salisbury Plain by the Devil himself. Another story has it as the creation of the wizard Merlin, as a burial site for Uther Pendragon, father of King Arthur, while a third has it as the marker of a Saxon massacre of the native British population.

All false, undoubtedly. But the devil, magic, and the conflict between Saxon, Norman, and Celt are all deeply intertwined with the history of Stonehenge.

But the reason for these myths is that Stonehenge itself is a mystery. There is no record of its creation, which was long before the written word came to Britain, and even the stories of the Druids, who are said by many to have been the stone circle's human creators, come from three millennia after the stones themselves were placed on Salisbury plain. The time between the stones' erection and those Roman tales is a greater distance than that between Caesar and our own time.

There are, of course, conjectures that can be made as to its purpose, but few of those suggested – use as a calendar, for example – would have justified the superhuman effort involved in transporting those stones, some weighing fifty tons or more, for dozens or hundreds of miles. These stones were not moved merely to act as a sundial – and if that had been their purpose, there were stones which were much closer which could have served the purpose just as easily.

No, the idea that this was merely created as a reminder of the seasons is, if anything, more fanciful than the tales about the Devil and Merlin.

There are more powerful magickal spots in England, certainly, but they are secrets, known only to the adept, and their existence is hidden from those who do not have the power to seek them out by themselves. And in a war of ideas, a secret battlefield may as well not exist.

So it was to this, the centre of magickal Britain, that Turing, Fleming, and Wheatley were approaching. There they saw, dressed all in white, Keynsham and his followers. They were re-enacting the death of Baldur, in the hope that their sacrifice would be resurrected as a god.

"The blasphemy! The sheer blasphemy!" muttered Wheatley under his breath.

"Oh come now," replied Turing. "Surely you know enough about the tradition of the dying and raising god to know that they're not mocking Christianity. Haven't you read Frazer?"

"Sir, I read Frazer while you were a foetus. It's not blasphemy against Christ I am objecting to here, but against the Norse gods. Any honestly-held faith is a source of the light, and should not be mocked."

"But surely a religion has to be either true or false? Either Christ was God incarnate, died, and was resurrected, or not. Either Mohammed was given the Koran by Allah, or not. These are questions which are susceptible to historical investigation."

"And does that apply to Newton's laws?"

"Beg pardon?"

Wheatley smiled. "Sir Isaac Newton. You may have heard of him?"

"Of course I have. Don't patronise me. What's your point?"

"My point is, Alan, that Newton proclaimed his laws as being absolute truth, much as those who preach from the Bible do. Yet I read that Herr Einstein's theories show that Newton was mistaken. Yet apples still fall from trees."

"So you're saying. . ."

"That truth and falsehood are not so important as the simple practicalities of the matter. No doubt Baldur or Christ never really existed, just as no doubt Newton was mistaken about gravity. But blasphemy against any honest religion merely because it is false will have similar results to sticking one's head in a guillotine, reasoning that as gravity is false the blade shall never fall."

Fleming asked "So are you saying that there is no absolute truth at all? There must be *some* straightforward answer to the question 'is there a God?', surely?"

"No, I see what he's saying," replied Turing. "There *are* questions which have no answer, or which have an answer we can never possibly discover."

"Indeed," said Wheatley, "and so we can never discover the answer to the question 'is Baldur real?', and nor should we want to, for it would spoil the mystery of life. But we *can* have an answer to the simpler question 'does Baldur *represent* something real?', and the answer to that question is of course an emphatic 'yes!', for all true religion contains within it a kernel of truth. And it is blasphemy against that kernel which upsets me."

Fleming didn't understand, but he sensed that he would get no explanation that satisfied him any better, and decided to leave the subject. Enough to know that Wheatley and Turing now seemed, at last, to be in some sort of agreement. Now he had to hope that that agreement could extend to a plan of action to destroy the enemy.

"Now we've got that sorted out," he said, exasperated, "perhaps we could now do something to prevent this atrocious act from taking place?"

There were twenty men in the stone circle in front of them, and there was no way that the three of them could overpower the cultists. Turing had to hope that the magickal workings by Crowley and the others would give them a hand. But right now, there was only one thing to do.

"We have to distract them, even if it means our own lives. If we can disrupt the ritual, we may yet succeed."

The three men marched forward, in the open, and the air around them seemed to crackle as they crossed the threshold of the circle.

The cultists turned toward them, daggers raised.

Chapter 35

Above the material plane on which the battle was taking place, was another plane altogether – and the old magickal truism of "as above, so below" applied here as much as anywhere. The events below were affecting the events on the astral plane, which in turn were affecting the material events unfolding below.

Throughout the structure of reality, ripples and intersections from different planes were affecting each other. The battle being fought was for the soul of England, and thus for the British Empire, but it was also a fight over worldviews, over modes of existence for the universe itself, over which gods would rule and which devils become allies.

Many magickal practitioners question whether the astral plane exists in "reality", or if it just exists in their minds, but those like Crowley who had spent decades learning how to manipulate reality to their own ends knew that this was the wrong question to be asking. The universe is much more complicated than the human brain can ever comprehend, but the universe *that a human being perceives* is all we can ever know.

So changing the universe is precisely and exactly the same thing as changing one's own perceptions of the universe. As above, so below – and as internally, so externally.

What mattered was not whether the astral plane was "real", but whether actions taken on that plane could affect the material plane. And long experience had convinced Crowley that they could and did.

Driberg had long been left behind by the other two. While he had sufficient knowledge of Crowley's magickal practices to achieve transcendence to the astral plane, he was far less able a mage than Knight, let alone Crowley, and he had found himself simply unable to keep up. While the others progressed on to higher planes, Driberg found himself keeping guard over their physical forms, a connection between the ethereal and material realms of existence.

Crowley and Knight were still in combat on the astral plane with the bestial demon creature being summoned by Keynsham. It seemed almost as if the demon was trying to distract them from something, although its rage seemed sincere enough. The creature was moving higher and higher into the sky, further away from the ground – as if it was trying to lead them away from the physical plane, into the higher astral planes where it was on its home ground.

And Horus followed it, flying at the creature, his beaks and talons tearing at it and causing blood-like liquid to fly from the wounds. The god and the demon may both be immortal and immaterial, but they were acting for all the world as if they were incarnate, with a physical presence.

The onlookers didn't know what kind of demon was being summoned, but they did know that Horus, in his aspect as Ra-Hoor-Khuit, was a god of the sun, and fire, and of war – a being made of pure elemental energy, who would destroy his enemies with the fury of atoms being torn into pieces.

This was, once again, the story of the war between light and darkness, between creation and decay – yet the creation embodied by Ra-Hoor-Khuit was a furious, all-consuming creation, one that produced light and heat but which destroyed everything that came close to it. It was a creation born of destruction – but of a magnificent destruction.

Horus the crowned and conquering child, an embodiment of entropy and rebirth, a firebird, a war hawk...that Horus was going to destroy anything and everything that stood in the way of its new creation, a creation which would be horrible in its beauty, and awesome in its horror. Ra-Hoor-Khuit might, at other times, have taken any side in the war – the political concerns of humans were none of his – but the demon conjured up by Keynsham embodied everything that Horus was not.

Where Ra-Hoor-Khuit embodied a cleansing fire, Keynsham's demon embodied putrefaction – an apparent stasis that hid a rot within, an apple that appeared ripe until the first bite, when one could see the maggots inside. Neither were, in our human conceptions, "good" or "evil", but they were opposites nonetheless, and Horus could no more refrain from opposing the demon than he could choose non-existence.

The Horus hawk shrieked in fury, and jets of flame shot from its mouth as it swooped down towards the stinking, rotting demon-thing, which might have been conjured up by Hess but which was now acting entirely on its own motives. The fire singed the demon and, where it touched, a light brighter than anything any human had ever seen, shone out for a brief moment.

The demon whirled and shrieked, clawing at the Horus hawk, but in vain. Every time it made contact with the god, the demon seemed to become more infuriated, as if its attacks were turned back against itself and it was being wounded by its own struggles. The hawk let out triumphant cries, as the demon screamed in utter fury.

Crowley and Knight watched, in awe, as every attack against the hawk seemed to make it grow brighter, seemed to make its purpose clearer. The Horus hawk now almost seemed to fill the sky, and the demon seemed to shrink, becoming less menacing and more ridiculous with every passing second. Soon it would be destroyed.

Whatever the true name of the demon – call it Moloch, call it Baal, or call it by some other name, it matters not – it could only do its work in the darkness, and the brightness of Ra-Hoor-

Khuit's flame was going to burn it away into nothingness.

Down below, they could see the cultists stopping in their approach on Turing, Wheatley, and Fleming. The cultists fell to their knees, screaming, as the demon drained power from them, using them up in order to sustain its own battle. Soon the cultists were silent – unconscious or dead, it was impossible to tell, but their spiritual energy had been used up. Even that, though, wasn't enough to keep the demon from shrinking and decaying.

But then Crowley and Knight saw that their own physical bodies were being approached – Keynsham had sent attackers to kill them while they were in a trance.

Chapter 36

Crowley and Knight were dejected. They knew now that Keynsham's plan was, short of a miracle, unstoppable. If their own bodies were to be destroyed, they would die along with them and be unable to prevent the demon's triumph, while were they to return to them and defend their physical forms, the demon would be able to proceed unmolested. But it was a choice between the tiny chance of success should they survive, and the non-existent chance should their physical bodies be left undefended.

There was only one thing for it – they would have to banish Horus, return to their bodies, and take the battle to the physical plane. They had lost their most potent weapon against Keynsham's ritual, and they just had to hope that less efficacious weapons would suffice.

The god-form of Horus disappeared in a blink, leaving nothing behind but a vague sense of something missing, as Crowley and Knight's attention turned from the war against the demon conjured by Keynsham to the practical matter of preserving their own bodies.

The demon howled in triumph and rose into the air, soaring and spinning around, knowing its victory was at hand. The stench of sulphur suffused the atmosphere, as its wings spread to their full extent, casting a shadow over the whole stone circle below as the demon screamed its furious joy.

But there was nothing they could do. They hadn't the time

to destroy the demon entirely before their own bodies fell victim to their attackers. Their choice was to sacrifice themselves, and slow but not stop the demon, or to stay alive and hope for some other means of success to present itself.

Leaving the demon to head towards the stones again, Crowley and Knight turned all their will towards moving as swiftly as they could back towards the material plane, where Driberg had already returned.

The demon was now feeding on the mental energy of the man who was to have been sacrificed. Even though the cultists had collapsed, the young man on the bluestone, who had more energy than any of them, was losing his life force to feed the destruction.

Turing, Fleming and Wheatley tried in vain to move the sacrifice away from the stones, but the force field was too strong.

"He won't budge!" cried Turing, "The silly bugger just won't move! Doesn't he realise what will happen to him if we don't get him out of the circle?"

"I'm sure he realises all too well. He wishes to abnegate his own self, to become part of the great darkness," replied Wheatley.

"How? How could anyone want such a fate for themselves?"

"Is it that different from the Buddhist concept of *nibbana*? The Buddha says the highest goal is non-existence, becoming one with the light side of the universe. He wants the same, for the darkness."

While this was happening, the men were still trying to tug the victim away, but even had the victim offered his assistance, rather than mutely resisting any attempts to save him, a force stronger than any of them seemed to be holding him down immobile. Try as they might, they could not get the sacrificial victim to move.

Turing looked down at the young man who was lying on the bluestone, and realised that this young man was going to die if Turing didn't save him.

Then at the last moment, a sudden change – light blue, electric, sparks started to fly from the stones. A smell of ozone permeated the air, and Turing felt every hair on his entire body stand on end. Sparks started appearing near the ground, and black, heavy clouds rolled in, centring on the giant stone which was being used for the sacrifice. The victim came to his senses, and the Nazis collapsed to the ground, apparently dead. Wheatley screamed, and he too collapsed.

Turing and Fleming pulled the sacrificial victim away from the bluestones, and collapsed on the ground, face first, physically drained and helpless to move any further. Turing gasped and wheezed, and with the last of his energy managed to roll onto his back, and start taking deeper breaths. He looked over at the other two.

Fleming was groaning softly, but Wheatley had stopped breathing – the effort had been too much for the older man, who was slowly turning purple. Turing called on reserves of energy of which he had previously been unaware, and managed to crawl over to Wheatley. He tried desperately to remember how one resuscitates someone who has stopped breathing.

But then, suddenly, Wheatley sat up.

"My God!" Turing exclaimed, "I thought for a moment that you were dead!"

"I was," said Wheatley. "I...no, I cannot explain what I experienced, but my body did die for a time. My spirit departed from it, and I cannot say I am entirely happy to have returned."

"Well, whether you're happy or not, I certainly am. We've still got to get this gentleman out of the area, and I shall need your assistance in carrying him. That is, if you're in any state to be able to help?"

"I shall survive, I believe. Just give me a few moments to catch my breath."

Turing rolled back onto his back, and the four men lay there for a few minutes, looking at the slowly-brightening sky, and at the dead bodies around them. There on the dewy grass lay the people who, mere seconds earlier, had been alive and well, planning to perform a human sacrifice and to kill anyone who got in their way. They might look unharmed, until one realised that they were no longer breathing.

Wheatley was unable to understand what had just happened. They'd been seconds away from death, and then suddenly their attackers were strewn about them. What could have caused this?

He knew he had been. . . somewhere else. Something had happened in that stone circle which could not be explained in any of the philosophies he had read. He might spend the rest of his life looking for an explanation, but knew it might still remain a mystery.

He looked over at Turing, who smiled back knowingly.

Chapter 37

As the rolls of thunder faded away, the clouds cleared to reveal the almost-risen sun, and the electrical charge in the air dissipated, Turing realised that the immediate danger, at least, was over. A grin spread across his face, and he managed to raise himself to his elbows. Sweat dripping from the locks of hair falling over his forehead, he was finally able to speak. He turned to Wheatley.

"Do you know, I wasn't at all sure that would work?"

"What do you mean?"

"I rewrote the ritual. Only slightly, but it seemed to me to be isomorphic to a circuit, so..."

"Oh, speak English, man!"

"The ritual was... analogous, that's probably the right word. It was analogous to some things in some of the mathematics I'm working on."

"What do you mean?"

"Mathematics is all about patterns. I've trained myself, my entire life, to be able to see patterns where others can't. That's what makes me able to... I'm sorry, I just realised I was going to reveal something I really shouldn't, about the nature of my current work. But suffice to say, when I saw the documents Hess had brought over, I saw patterns in there."

"All right. So what did you do?"

"Well, there was a logical flow of ideas, like a mathematical proof or the flow of electricity in a circuit. You only have to change one thing — in this case a single syllable — to make the flow go the other way. What I did, essentially, was to change one phrase from saying 'you will' to 'you will not'. That's all."

"That's *all*? Have you any idea what it was that you did?"

"Yes. What I did was prevent the ritual from working. I rather thought that was a good thing."

"Oh you did, did you? And what if your 'you will not' had been aimed at the universe? What if you made it say 'you will not continue to exist'?"

"Oh don't be absurd."

"Absurd? Have you any idea of the forces with which you were meddling? The terrible, catastrophic, results if you had been wrong?"

"No. No I haven't. And the reason I have no idea of those forces is because I was brought into a battle and not given the most basic information."

Wheatley glared at him. "All the more reason, then, not to interfere with anything outside your area of knowledge. The whole reason we're in this mess is because of fellows like you sticking their nose into matters that they don't understand. I swear if I told you 'this button will blow up the world' you'd press it just to see what happened."

"Yes, I very well might. Because I don't think anyone would be damn fool enough to *make* a button that could blow up the world, but they might well want to make me *think* they'd made such a button, so I wouldn't press it. And I would want to know what it was that they didn't want me to know."

Fleming sighed. "Alan, you still have a lot to learn about human nature if that's really what you think. Not only are there men who are precisely that foolish, there are men who would make it *and then press it themselves*, just to prove to themselves that they could do it."

"You're a cynic, Ian. People are basically good, when you get right down to it, you know. People do horrid things some-times, no doubt, but in my experience there are very few horrid people."

"Hmm. I'd like to think you were right. But in my own experience, people are venal, nasty shits."

"I can't believe you really think that way."

"I do. I absolutely do."

"But then... but then why on Earth do you work so hard trying to save them, if you think so poorly of them? Why not just give up and let the Nazis do their worst? Why bother?"

Fleming smiled, but said nothing.

The man who had been intended as the ritual sacrifice, who had been lying unconscious for much of this time, let out a groan. Turing knelt down by him, his face suddenly showing concern.

"Are you all right there? Do you know where you are?"

The sacrifice looked up. "I'm... I'm alive? I was meant to be in paradise by now. What went wrong? Why am I still in my body?"

"I'm afraid to inform you," said Fleming, "that your ritual was not a success. However, you have one consolation."

"What?"

"I strongly suspect that after a short trial for treason, you shall be leaving your body behind as you planned, although it will be at the end of the hangman's rope, rather than a magician's knife."

Turing turned to glare at Fleming. "You really think now is the time to be talking about hanging this poor man? You're a disgrace. We just saved his life!"

"And no-one is more annoyed at that turn of events than I. The man's a traitor, and should be treated as such."

"A traitor?! He's little more than a boy, and we have no evidence that he was a volunteer! They were going to slit the man's throat, Ian!"

Wheatley looked at the two squabbling friends, his face grim. "Whether he is a traitor, a fool, or a victim, is surely for the courts to decide. For now, we still have work to do."

The friends, and the man they had grudgingly saved, made their way back to the cars they had abandoned earlier, and to their occultist colleagues. They had to hope that now the magickal ritual had been ended, whatever force had prevented them from driving to Stonehenge would allow them to make their way to London unimpeded.

The dew glinted in the dawn as they trudged across the fields.

Chapter 38

But Keynsham's ritual hadn't been completely unsuccessful. It had sent the "go" signal for Germany's attack on Russia.

The Molotov-Ribbentrop pact was now over. Germany had been massing its troops and tanks on the border of the USSR for some time, but Stalin had refused to believe that they were going to break the neutrality agreement, especially after Russia had also pledged neutrality in the Sino-Japanese war.

But in the early hours of June 22, 1941, Operation Barbarossa began. Against the advice of his generals, and against all common sense, Hitler decided now was the time to fight his greatest foe – the "Jewish Bolshevism" he believed would destroy the "Aryan" race. The tanks rolled in, and Germany was now at war on two fronts.

Everything Hitler had done up to that point had gone the way he had wished, and he had now become convinced that this pattern would continue, and that the German people were truly invincible. He would soon be shown that this was very far from the truth. The attack on the USSR would be the start of Germany's defeat.

Keynsham had planned that his ritual would force Britain to ally with Germany against the Communist menace. But Turing's changes had reversed that. Now Britain would ally with Russia against the Germans.

The German high command, though, were unaware of this. As far as they were concerned, all they had to do was to attack

the USSR and the British Empire would immediately realise
that the Germans were on the same side. After all, hadn't the
Soviets killed the Czar – the cousin of the present British King?
Surely a defeat of the Soviets would be more important to them
than continuing a fight that had, after all, started over Poland,
of all unimportant places?

They couldn't have been more wrong. Before the magickal
rite, the British Government had been determined to smash
the Nazi regime utterly, and to see Hitler, Goebbels, Göring,
and the rest dead. That determination had been redoubled by
Turing's alteration of the instructions. Now even if it meant
the destruction of the British Empire itself, Germany *would* be
destroyed.

Everything that followed in the war – the siege of Stalingrad,
the long, slow defeat of the German army at the expense of
millions of Russian lives, the eventual conquest of Germany by
the Allied forces as the Germans discovered they couldn't fight
on two fronts – all followed from this.

Had Keynsham lived to see the results of his work, he would
have been unimaginably horrified. His dream of uniting the
Aryan race and crushing the Communists was dead forever.
But he was saved from having to see the country he claimed
to love but which he betrayed allying with the people he most
despised.

Keynsham had, however inadvertently, shaped the entire
history of the world. He would leave an enormous legacy –
one of war, disaster, and a world divided, but one that was
nonetheless possibly the least-worst of all possible worlds given
the situation in 1941. The fact that he would have loathed this
legacy, and never intended it, did not make that any less the
case.

Of course, none of those at Stonehenge in the early hours
of that fateful morning knew that this would be the result of
Turing's actions. For all they knew, the effect had merely been
a localised one, and the deaths of the Nazis in the stone circle

had not affected the plan.

Indeed, as far as Crowley, Knight, and Driberg knew, the deaths had been part of the occultists' plan, and it was entirely possible that the Nazis' spirits had transcended mortal form and gained the powers of gods. They had no reason to hope for any better.

And yet hope they did. Something seemed to have changed, and while none of them knew what that thing was, they could all tell that the world seemed lighter.

Crowley slowly stood up, having apparently aged a decade in a matter of minutes. The battle had taken its toll spiritually, and the mental effort with which he had projected an appearance of strength and solidity was too much for him now. He looked again like a frail old man.

"I think," he said, slowly, the effort of every word showing on his face, "that we have succeeded in our task. We have been very lucky here. We have done something today. It may not have been enough to make the difference in the war, but more by luck than skill we have done *something*."

Driberg nodded, and pointed towards the stone circle in the distance, where he could see the figures of Turing, Wheatley, Fleming, and another man he didn't recognise, slowly walking towards them.

"It would appear so. At the very least, our men appear to have survived, which is a good sign."

As Turing, Wheatley, Fleming, and the other man approached, Driberg realised that they must have been through something similar to his own experiences. Like Crowley and, as Driberg now understood, like himself, they all looked older than they had mere minutes earlier. Whether what they'd experienced could truly compare to his own astral flight, Driberg didn't know, but he knew they had struggled similarly.

Fleming was smiling, despite the deep weariness on his face. "You three have a good nap while we were saving the country?" he said in a light-hearted tone.

Crowley smiled back. "I suspect our mental exertions may have had more effect than your physical ones. Nonetheless, whoever contributed most, our collaboration has yielded results, and for that we may all be grateful."

They made their way back to their cars in silence.

Chapter 39

It was a few months later that Crowley and Wheatley met up again, for the first time – other than during the Hess incident – since their brief acquaintance in the thirties. Crowley was even more physically frail than he had been in June, and Wheatley suspected that he didn't have a great deal of time left to live. The two of them sat down together over a glass of brandy (in Wheatley's case) and half a bottle of absinthe (in Crowley's).

"I must apologise again for calling you a traitor, Mr. Crowley. That was completely uncalled for."

"Oh, there are far worse things to be called, and I have been called almost all of them. Were I the kind of man who allowed himself to be hurt by the opinions of polite society, I should never have become who I am today."

"But still, an accusation of treachery is not one that should be made as lightly as I did."

"Oh, I'm sure in your own eyes I am a traitor. At the very least, I am likely responsible for the last war, and so indirectly for this one."

"How on Earth could you be responsible for the last war?"

"Well, possibly not responsible myself. But I was the conduit through which the Book of the Law came. And I performed. . . various rituals as a result of the dawning of the Aeon of Horus, and those rituals undoubtedly started the last war. There's no doubt in my mind about that."

Wheatley shifted in his seat. "But even if that is the case, you didn't cause this war."

"Not cause, no. But I have strong suspicions that my writings were influential upon people I should not want to consider my intellectual children. Take, for example the Thule society. 'Thule' is only one letter different, kabbalistically, from Thelema. But that letter makes all the difference. Thelema brings about the aeon of the conquering child. But Thule... Thule has a kabbalistic value of 444. That is the value of 'dam shafach' in Hebrew."

"I'm sorry, I don't know Hebrew."

"It means 'shed blood'. As in Leviticus 17:4. 'blood shall be imputed unto that man; he hath shed blood; and that man shall be cut off from among his people'."

"So these Thule Society people..."

"Are the force behind the Nazis. Idiot meddlers, lost in the abyss, who have lost the spirit of scientific enquiry that animates all true magi, and fallen prey to the worst of superstition; so lost in darkness they deny even the possibility of light."

Wheatley thought for a moment.

"I would have thought you'd be all for a bit of darkness, Crowley."

"Oh, one has to have a *bit* of darkness, yes. It livens one up no end. But there's a difference between a little darkness and an end to all light. My system is, after all, a very moderate one."

"Your 'system' is still evil, you know. And I have every intention of telling the world so. Just because for once you did the right thing – for whatever twisted reason – I won't believe that you are not on the side of Satan."

"Oh, I think Satan is a most misunderstood person, and I have every sympathy for him. But I intend to replace him, not take his side."

"Replace him?"

"Oh yes. He's not doing the job properly, assuming he even exists. I mean look at the world. He's more interested in petty nastinesses than in real power. Imagine what someone with a brain could do with his resources."

"Your hubris really knows no bounds, does it?"

Crowley took another sip of his absinthe and then smiled, his teeth seeming somehow sharper than they had a second earlier.

"My dear Dennis, *hubris* is merely the slaves' name for the natural human desire to be the master. A man who knows his own will accepts the wish to become God as a reasonable prerequisite for achieving anything worthwhile. I should hardly wish to be a puppet if instead I can be the puppeteer."

Wheatley sipped his brandy. "I take your point, of course. But one has to accept reality. There is a hierarchy. There are inferiors and superiors, and we each have our superiors just as our inferiors do. Promote a man above his station, and the most dreadful results will undoubtedly follow."

"Oh, I couldn't agree more. Imagine the frightful mess were a policeman to be set free of the laws that bind him. Such inferior types must be kept in their restraints, to protect the rest of us from their folly. I merely believe that such rules do not apply to those like myself capable of breaking them."

Wheatley frowned. "And this is, I think, where we differ the most. Rules are not made to be broken, Mr. Crowley – they are made to be kept, and must apply to all equally if they are to mean anything at all. What you advocate is nothing more nor less than the purest anarchy. It's outright Bolshevism, and I won't stand for it."

"Sometimes Bolshevism is better than the alternative, though I have to admit that I am no lover of the Bolshevik system. But there are worse. Which reminds me, Mr. Wheatley. The letter you sent me several years ago, in which you sang the praises of Herr Hitler. . . I have to inform you of a terrible error on my part. I was throwing some useless scraps onto the fire, and I accidentally threw your letter along with them. It is, I am afraid, quite, quite, destroyed."

Wheatley blinked. "I'm quite sure I have no memory of such a letter. Sounds like some forger has conned you. I certainly hope you didn't give him any money. But thank you anyway — the existence of a letter like that, even a forged one, could have had unfortunate consequences."

He stood up and extended his hand to Crowley. Crowley took it and smiled. The two men turned, and went their separate ways, neither looking back.

Chapter 40

Life had returned to normal at Bletchley Park – or at least, as close to normal as it gets at a secret military intelligence base decoding encrypted messages that the enemy thinks are unbreakable, and when every decision may mean life or death for thousands of people.

But even that kind of work can, in the end, turn out to be just another job, just something to get through in order to survive.

There had, of course, been an increase in the volume of transmissions to be decrypted as a result of the German invasion of Russia, and the Huts were busier than ever in their work, but Alan Turing was once again itching for a new challenge, for something to break the monotony.

He was whistling "Whistle While You Work" to himself, half-consciously, to try to cheer himself up, while looking through another batch of paperwork, and didn't notice Ian Fleming walk into the office and stand over him, until Fleming spoke.

"What's that?"

"Sorry? Oh, hello Ian. I didn't see you there."

"You were whistling."

"Was I? Yes, I probably was. I do quite a lot."

"But I thought. . ."

"Yes?"

"So you *can* whistle?"

"Er. . . yes. Why do you ask?"

"Oh, no reason. I just thought. . . never mind."

Turing raised an eyebrow. Fleming was a confusing person, but then so were most people. He decided that whatever Fleming was driving at, it wasn't worth trying to figure it out, so he dismissed it.

"So, what brings you back to Bletchley?"

"Nothing I can talk about right now, I'm afraid. How's the code-breaking going?"

"Likewise."

"Hmm."

"I should think it'll be settling down soon enough, though. The war seems to slowly be turning a corner. There'll be less and less for us to do."

"Oh, I don't know. I suspect there's a few more years yet."

"I suppose so. Depressing."

Fleming talked about wanting to be a writer like Wheatley after the war, but Turing advised him against it.

"No-one wants to read about espionage and infiltration. I mean, yes, the things we've just done, they might, but not the normal day-to-day stuff."

"Oh, I don't know. I think there might be a few people who want to read about espionage. But how about yourself? What will you do, once the war's at an end?"

"Oh, the same kind of thing, I suppose. Work on logical problems. Possibly work further on using electronics to solve mathematical problems."

The two men sat together for a while, not saying anything to each other, just thinking about their own future plans. Fleming was the first to break the silence.

"Do you ever think. . ."

"What?"

"Nothing."

"No, come on."

"Well, I was just wondering about the things we saw. Do you think they were real gods and demons?"

"What I think is that I don't have a reasonable definition of the words 'gods' or 'demons'. I think they were something, certainly, but whether they were purely our imagination, they have some sort of corporeal form, or. . . something else. . . well, *hypotheses non fungo*. I'll have to collect more evidence before I make my mind up."

"That doesn't seem like much of an answer to me."

"It's the best answer I can give. Sometimes things don't have a simple answer. Sometimes, in fact, it's impossible for us even to know if there *is* an answer or not. In this case, I suspect there is, and one day I may be able to discover it. Until then, I just have to acknowledge my ignorance."

Fleming looked at Turing, a curious expression on his face.

"Your mind really doesn't work the same way everyone else's does, does it?"

"Oh, I have no idea. How can we ever really know how another's mind works? All we have to go on are the surfaces. We never get to see what's going on underneath."

Fleming looked over at the radiator, and saw Turing's mug chained there.

"Alan, do you mind if I ask you a question? Why *do* you keep that mug chained up? Surely the theft of a mug that couldn't cost more than sixpence wouldn't inconvenience you all that greatly?"

Turing smiled. "If you lock up only those things you don't mind being stolen, you convince thieves that anything not locked up isn't worth stealing."

Fleming grinned. "You're a devious little bugger underneath that boyish exterior, aren't you?"

"Oh, I don't know. I just think about things a little more than most people bother to. One only has to think one step ahead to appear a genius, you know."

"And how many steps ahead *do* you think?"

Turing smiled. "One more than you."

The two men shook hands. Nothing more needed to be said

between them, and nothing more seemed likely to. There was still a war to be fought, but both were aware that the greatest danger had now passed, and that while millions more would lose their lives, those losses would likely not be in vain.

Fleming left, and Turing turned back to his work.

There was always more to do, and any break in his activity had to be a short one. There would be time enough for rest when the war was over, although Turing suspected that even then there would always be something calling on his time.

But for now, he had a simple task in front of him, and it was one he could perform almost mechanically. He could allow his mind to wander while his body continued its task, and he could be sure that his body would perform its task adequately without mental supervision.

Somewhere in the distance, Turing thought he could hear an eagle scream. He looked up to the sky, but saw nothing, other than a darkening red sky that spoke of a thunderstorm still to come. He took another sip of his tea, and he returned to work.

Printed in Great Britain
by Amazon